To Pancho -

from Yo

Best Wishes!

John McLaughlin

I shall be telling this with a sigh
Somewhere ages and ages hence:
Two roads diverged in a wood, and I,
I took the one less traveled by,
And that has made all the difference.

-Robert Frost, "The Road Not Taken"

Library of Congress Control Number: 20011917335

Published by John McLaughlin Books
Peoria, Arizona
www.johnmclaughlinbooks.com

Published by John McLaughlin Books 2012
Printed by Lightning Source Inc. (US)
Cover and interior art work by Jonathan McLaughlin (jonmclaughlin.com)

Printed in the United States of America
978-0-615-54518-9

Dedicated to

All Veterans and Scout Dogs
Who served America during the Vietnam War

With a Very Special Thanks to
Joe Darrell Lovelace, Sergeant
50th Infantry Platoon, 4th Infantry Division
And
Buck, Infantry Platoon Scout Dog

ACKNOWLEDGEMENTS

I would like to express my heart-felt thanks to Joe Darrell Lovelace, who provided his Vietnam War experience as a Scout Dog Handler from February, 1967 through March, 1968. This invaluable experience and knowledge, which at times was uncomfortable for Sergeant Lovelace in the re-telling, provided an accurate accounting of military service and the war for the author's use as background for the main character, Jack Wetzel, in this story of fiction. Also, I extend a special thanks to Joe's wife Vicki for assisting Joe, and ultimately the author, to talk about a violent and sometimes best forgotten time in his young life.

This fictional story with fictional characters is not about Sergeant Lovelace, but rather a story of any of the many men and women who much like Joe served their country when they were called. And, it is a story worth telling of their stalwart, furry companions —the scout dogs.

Also, thanks to the legendary Frank Smith, real-life New Mexico Department of Game and Fish Officer from the Heart Bar Ranch for his assistance.

John D. McLaughlin

AUTHOR'S NOTE

During the Vietnam War, 2,709,918 Americans served in uniform with more than 58,000 members of the United States Armed Forces losing their lives and more than 300,000 wounded.

The U.S. military deployed about 4,300 dogs to combat zones between 1965 and 1973.

According to the military, 281 dogs died in the line of duty, but hundreds more died when the war ended and the U.S. troops departed. It has been estimated that military dogs saved about 10,000 lives in Vietnam. In those years, there were no provisions for military dogs to be adopted. Most were euthanized or left behind to uncertain fates.

DISCLAIMER

The characters in this book are ficticious, and any resemblance, living or dead, is purely doggoned coincidental.

IN THE SHADOW OF THE MOUNTAIN

A Novel

By

John D. McLaughlin

CHAPTER ONE
Mimbres Valley, New Mexico
Present Day

The old dog moved slowly in the bed of the truck toward the tailgate as his master exited the driver's door. Although well past middle age, the man walked lithely, his tall slender frame outpacing his companion in the bed of the '51 Chevy. As he lowered the heavy tailgate and secured each side, the dog made it to the rear of the truck; the tired eyes looked up at his master of many years. A smile formed on the dog's haggard face, his tail wagged.

"Wel-l-l now, Wally. I reckon you want me to lift you down, uh?" The old man smiled back at the dog, gently petting the Australian Sheppard then rubbing behind his ears. Sitting beside the dog on the tailgate, the man reached up and tipped his stained and battered Stetson back on his head with his thumb. "I know all about arthritis, boy. I reckon I got it bad, too. I had a helluva time just gettin' outta bed this mawnin'."

The dog edged closer to the man, placed his front paws then his head in the man's lap. The old man sighed as he rubbed the dog's ears again. It was fall in New Mexico, and the Mimbres Valley had lost its summer lushness, a dreary brown replacing bright green alluding to the cold weather that would surely follow. Dusk descended over the valley as the man and dog silently watched together. The Black Range with its dark, towering mountain range accentuated the far horizon. As the shadow of the mountain drew nearer, a cool breeze rustled the mostly leafless cottonwood trees near the small adobe house that sat a quarter mile off Highway 35.

The clear sky began to bristle with stars; a lonely coyote howled out in the stillness of the night. Moments later, other coyotes responded. The old man's weather-beaten face broke into a smile again as he said softly to himself, "Thank you, God ... for another day. Me an' ol' Wally, why, we surely thank ya." The man wore a faded denim jumper over a blue and red flannel work shirt, faded jeans, and a pair of worn White's Packer boots.

They sat there, the old man and the much older dog, enjoying the quiet of the night and each other's company. The dog stirred beside his master, his ears perked. Then the old man heard the truck long before he saw the headlights. It turned off Highway 61 then accelerated fast heading north on Highway 35. As the vehicle approached, he heard the music and voices. *Damned loud mouths and their rock music!* Irritated, he shook his head and thought a man can't even enjoy the quietness of the evening.

The big truck skidded to a stop after sliding sideways near the entrance to his graveled driveway. The headlight's beam cast a bright light well ahead of the vehicle. It sliced a path through the dark night illuminating the highway. Where the road curved ahead, the huge nearly naked cottonwood trees billowed in the breeze on the east side of the Mimbres River.

A man cursed loudly in Spanish then English. A truck door creaked as it was opened and glass bottles shattered as they hit the pavement. The metal door creaked again and slammed shut, shattering the quiet of the night once again. The old man slipped off the tailgate, his eyes narrowed as he peered intently toward the truck parked at the entrance to his driveway. He saw a man urinating in front of the headlights and another man kicking at something near the driver's door. A high pitched yelp. More cursing. Another yelp from a dog.

The old man walked softly to the passenger side of the '51 Chevy truck, reached through an open window to the glove box and retrieved a Model 66 Smith & Wesson revolver. This he placed in his belt at his back and under the denim jumper. He turned to his dog. "You'd best stay here, Wally." As he started down the driveway, he said under his breath, "No need for both of us to deal with this sorry bunch, boy."

The old man pulled his Stetson down on his head as he strode toward the truck, his heavy boots crunching in the gravel. Within twenty feet of the truck, he clearly saw a young shirtless man who was in the process of kicking at an emaciated black and tan dog. The dog ducked and the drunk missed, almost falling to the ground. Multiple tattoos covered his arms, neck and back. A dirty ball cap adorned his head. "Come here, goddammit! You miserable cur." The dog disappeared around the rear of the truck, the man followed.

The old man's voice stopped him in his tracks. "Hold it, pard."

Tattoo turned, facing the old man, a beer bottle in his hand. He stared at the old man standing before him.

"What'd ya say to me?" There was insolence in the strained voice.

The old man took his time as he searched the darkness for the other man he had seen urinating earlier. The man appeared around the back of the truck and the old man turned slightly so that he could see both men. The second man's hair was shaved on both sides with a tuft of hair down the center Mohawk style. The hair, what there was of it, was colored red, green and yellow.

Tattoo stepped closer. The voice rose. "I asked you a friggin' question, you ol' bastard."

"I heard you," the old man answered quietly. "What's the matter with your dog?"

Mohawk spoke, "That ain't none o' your business, *cabrón*."

Tattoo took a long drink of his beer. "What's your name, ol' man?"

"Wetzel." The old man hooked his thumbs in the front pockets of his jeans.

Tattoo snorted. "Wetzel?" The insolence returned.

"That's right. Wetzel." The old man noted Mohawk moving closer. He looked Tattoo squarely in the eyes. His hazel eyes hardened but the voice was soft, "Why don't you just leave the dog?" He motioned toward the dog with his left hand. "He's just in your way. I'll care for him, and you boys can be on your way to the party."

Tattoo looked into the old man's eyes, his face twitched as he suddenly stepped back against the truck. Mohawk appeared alongside his friend and said, "Shut up, *viejo*!"

He advanced toward Wetzel then stopped, a crooked smile forming on his lips. He turned back toward the truck. "I'll show you what we do to *perros pendejos*." A semi-automatic pistol appeared in his hand. He walked to the other side of the truck and fired four shots in quick succession. The dog yelped. Silence.

Mohawk proudly returned. He held the pistol out with both hands as he crossed in front of the headlights. He looked for the old man where he had stood, but couldn't find him. A devilish grin was displayed on his drunken face. Laughing loudly, he said, "Hey, *viejo*. Come here! I'll show you what we do to *viejos pendejos*."

A quiet voice spoke from the darkness, "The only stupid person I see is an ugly lookin' parrot standing in front of his headlights." The voice came from a new location in the darkness. "Drop the gun. Now!"

Silence. His grin slowly vanished. Mohawk gripped the pistol tighter with both hands frantically searching the darkness for his prey. Two shots almost as one reverberated the quietness followed by another quick shot. Mohawk staggered back, falling to the pavement hit twice in the chest and once in the forehead.

The old man spoke sharply to Tattoo, "Get your hands up! Spread your fingers."

Tattoo dropped his beer bottle as he complied, the sound of the glass breaking against the pavement startling him. "Jesus Christ! Don't shoot me." He peered into the darkness, but couldn't see the old man. "I ain't armed."

"Turn around ... slowly." Tattoo turned in a circle, still unable to see the old man. The voice came from a slightly different location. "Down on the ground. *Now*!"

As Tattoo dropped to his hands and knees, he heard, "*Boca abajo. Separe los brazos, palmas arriba*." Tattoo lay face down with his arms out to his side, palms up as directed. Strong hands secured both his wrists within a leather belt loop that was tightened to secure his arms at his back. Competent hands searched him thoroughly for weapons.

The old man panted. "You move and I'll blow your damned head off. *Comprende?*"

Tattoo nodded without speaking. His eyes were wide and drool ran from his open mouth.

Gravel crunched. The old man walked over to the dead Mohawk. He quickly reloaded and placed his own revolver in the belt at his back and searched the dead man, finding no additional weapons. With a red handkerchief from the back pocket of his jeans he retrieved the semi-auto pistol lying on the ground. After making the pistol safe, he laid it on the hood and continued to the other side of the truck where the black and tan lay in a pool of blood. The old man sighed deeply. He reached down, patted the motionless dog and returned to the driver's side via the back of the truck. Tattoo lay on the ground as instructed.

The old man rubbed his jaw. He spoke to the Australian Sheppard limping slowly down the driveway, "I'm okay, Wally. You go on up to the house." He raised his arm and pointed toward the adobe house. The old dog turned and obediently started the slow journey back.

Wetzel withdrew a cell phone from his shirt pocket and dialed 9-1-1.

"Grant County Sheriff's Department." The female voice broke the stillness.

"Howdy, Stella. How ya been?"

Silence, then: "Wetzel? That you, Jack?"

"I reckon. Is Don at the office?"

"No. The sheriff rarely works late, and you shouldn't be using 9-1-1 unless you have an emergency. You know better, Jack."

Wetzel ignored the chastisement. "You'd best get a deputy out to my place. I've got a dead man and another sumbitch in custody in my driveway."

"*What*?

"You heard me. Get an officer rolling." Wetzel shifted the cell phone closer to his ear. "And get Don outta bed."

"You ... all right, Jack?"

"Yeah." He started to disconnect. "Tell Don if he's interested, there's a bunch of dope in the back of these guys' truck." He closed the cell phone and walked over to the prostrate Tattoo. "You do as you're told and rest easy. You'll be all right, son."

Tattoo whimpered and began sobbing.

The old man sat down, built a cigarette, taking his time. He stuck it in the corner of his mouth and lit it with a match from his jumper pocket. Drawing deeply on the cigarette, he thought about what had just transpired. It was never an easy task to take another man's life and even more difficult to live with it afterwards. *Dammit to hell!* Why hadn't he left them be to do whatever to the old hound dog? It wasn't right them being mean to the dog. But Jeez, he had no way of knowing they were dope-runners with a propensity for violence. It just wasn't right to be mean or abusive to any animal, including man.

He sat quietly, the cigarette tucked in the corner of his mouth. It glowed brightly in the darkness illuminating the faint outlines of a dark, wrinkled face then began a slow dance from one corner of his mouth to the other. The stars winked in a dark sky with a small sliver of the moon visible. Tattoo sobbed loudly then babbled incoherently. A cow bellowed out in the night. Wetzel sighed. For no reason, he thought of his life. *Christ, I'm sixty-two years old, and it's been a helluva ride for me, uh?* He drew again on the cigarette as he thought of a special person in his life. *Maggie, darlin'. I surely miss you!*

The mountain's dark shadow had lengthened to encompass where the old man stood. The present slowly faded away as Wetzel smoked and reminisced those years long ago. The cigarette continued its dance between his lips. He did not hear the two mule deer cross the gravel road behind him or Wally's short bark acknowledging their presence. Jack Wetzel's mind was elsewhere.

CHAPTER TWO
Silver City, New Mexico, 1966

The football was snapped. Jack Wetzel sprang forward and hit the defensive end across from him hard then ran an in-and-out pattern angling toward the sidelines. Sweat covered his flushed young face encased in the blue and silver football helmet. It ran down his neck, but he paid no mind as his cleated feet sprinted over the green turf. Turning, he looked for the football and saw it coming at him. *Too high!* Grunting, he leaped into the cold fall air; his arms stretched high, hands reaching frantically for the spiraling football that attempted to elude his grasp. He felt a Cobre High School defender slam against him as he arched high, twisting in mid-air. *Yes! I've got it.* His hands grasped the leather pigskin tightly as he fell backward. Suddenly, he was hit hard by another Cobre defender. The hit jarred his teeth and took his breath away as he catapulted in the air and landed on the frozen ground with a thud.

His vision dimmed, but he did see the referee in his black and white striped shirt and black ball cap, his arms raised, signaling a touchdown. The Silver High School Band blared out a response and the home crowd supporting the Silver High Colts football team roared its approval. As his best friend and quarterback Juan Garcia helped him to his feet, a sharp pain in his back almost doubled him over. Garcia shouted above the noise of the crowd, "We did it, Jackie, boy! We whipped 'em, by Golly."

Wetzel straightened slowly, grimacing with pain. Then

with effort he smiled at Garcia. "You bet, pard." He couldn't help thinking, *I've got chores to do early in the morning at the ranch, and it ain't goin' to be an easy task.*

***

Wetzel sat quietly on the bench in front of his opened football locker. The disheveled dark brown hair and sweaty, tired face told the story of his motionless half-dressed appearance. He had removed his heavy football shoes, his jersey bearing the blue number 89 along with the shoulder pads, but had failed to progress any further. A wet, soggy T-shirt clung to his slender frame.

Cleated feet approached to where he sat on the bench. Wetzel looked up and saw teammate Joe Peach standing over him. A burly, light-complected boy who Wetzel had beaten out for the starting end position, Peach had challenged him for the position last year as well as this, his senior year, but failed to compete for the job. Displaying his unhappiness at his own lack of success, he periodically made smart-aleck comments behind Wetzel's back. For the most part, Wetzel ignored him, realizing it was tough to lose out on what was important in life. He had talked the situation over with his mom on several occasions, and she agreed he had taken the best course of action.

Peach glared down at him. Wetzel returned the gaze. Although tired, he tried to keep the shortness out of his voice. "What is it, Joe?"

Grinning, Peach reached down and picked up one of Wetzel's football shoes and said, "Think you're pretty hot, don't ya?" Then he threw the heavy cleated shoe down the length of the locker room into the showers. Other football players already in the showers yelled out. His thin lips curled back from scraggly, unclean teeth as he sneered, "Well. Go on. *Fetch*, hot dog."

Wetzel sighed. His eyes hardened but he said nothing. He straightened his lanky frame, wincing as he did so, walked down to the shower and retrieved the wet shoe. Walking past Peach, he placed the shoe on the bench. As he turned toward the locker, Peach reached for the other shoe.

Wetzel's voice had a metallic edge to it. "Don't do it, Joe. You've had your fun. Now, move on!"

Peach grinned broadly while scanning the room to see if others would join him in his play. He picked up the shoe and cocked his arm to throw as Wetzel hit him square in the face with the retrieved wet football shoe. Peach's front teeth shattered and blood erupted from his mouth and nose as he went down to the floor like a pole-axed bull. Wetzel jumped astride him and continued beating him in the face with the heavy cleated shoe. His eyes wide with fright, Peach attempted to ward off the blows but Wetzel was too strong for him. He screamed, first in fright then for help, but the blood and broken teeth muffled his incoherent cries for help. He choked on the blood and debris in his mouth.

Strong arms encircled Wetzel and pulled him from the prostrate bully. "Easy, Jack. Easy now. It's me. Your buddy, Juan." Garcia continued to hold tightly to his friend's shoulders as he looked down at what had been a face and was now totally unrecognizable. "Geez, Jack," was all he could say.

Wetzel's blazing eyes dwindled to hard, black simmering coals as he dropped the bloody shoe with a loud clank on the cement floor of the locker room. He looked down at the frightened, bloody bully pointing at him. "You ... stay away from me," he choked, "or I'll break your damned neck." Between clenched teeth he struggled for enough air to speak. “You ignorant son-of-a-bitch.”

***

Maggie O’Brian sauntered down one of the many crowded hallways at Silver High School. Her bright red hair was pulled back into a pony tail and fastened with a single rubber band. The pony tail bounced from side to side as she walked, carrying an armload of books. Her pretty features were accentuated by bright green eyes and an honest face which easily broke into a warm smile. She wore a plain cotton red blouse with a full knee length pleated blue skirt. About her shoulders, a black sweater kept the fall coolness at a distance. On her slender ankles and tiny feet, she wore white cotton socks encased in brown penny loafer shoes.

She stopped at a set of lockers aligning the hallway where a tall, dark headed boy was retrieving books from his locker. Cheerfully, she hailed him, “Hi, Jack!”

He turned quickly, a smile appearing on his tanned face. “Maggie! How are ya, kid?” She smiled back thinking why in the world did this handsome guy not have a girlfriend? They had been close friends for many years as he and her boyfriend, Juan Garcia, were best pals. He was shy around most girls in school, but not with her. They were good friends and the three of them hung out together. She had met Jack Wetzel’s mother once and immediately liked her. A nice, hard-working ranch lady who had her husband taken away from her way too early in life. Jack’s dad had worked for the U.S. Forest Service in the Gila National Forest, and during the summer of 1955 had lost his life trying to save another crewmember on the Little Creek Fire.

Maggie knew that Jack worked at a part-time job helping the veterinarian in Arenas Valley, and the full-time job helping his mother work their small ranch to make ends meet. No doubt he didn’t have a lot of time to date girls.

Wetzel cocked his Stetson back on his head with his thumb. He was wearing a denim shirt and jumper and faded wrangler jeans with brown Roper boots. His thick brown hair curled out from under his hat. She'd heard other girls at school refer to his hazel eyes as "bedroom eyes". She didn't know about that for she only thought of him as a good friend, but she did know there was a kindness behind those eyes and Jack Wetzel was a good honest person.

Maggie shifted the heavy books in her arms. Wetzel stepped forward, reaching for the books. "Here, Maggie girl. Let me hold these for you." She reluctantly agreed.

"Where's Juan?" Wetzel slammed his locker shut with his elbow.

"He said to meet me at your locker." She looked down the hallway. A smile lit up her face. "Here he comes now, Jack."

Wetzel looked at her then smiled. "You like Juan a bunch, don't ya?"

Bright green eyes met somber hazel. She did not hesitate in answering, "I love him more than anything in the world, Jack." Eyes glowing, she watched as the tall Garcia approached them. He waved then shouted. A Hispanic, Garcia's handsome features included short curly black hair, dark complexion, broad shoulders and thick chest. He wore his high school letter jacket, blue and gray, the letter "S" on the front right breast bristling with football, basketball and track insignias.

"Hey, guys," he said as he strolled up. "How's my two favorite friends?

"*Bien, amigo,*" responded Wetzel.

Garcia slapped him on the back while he patted Maggie's shoulder affectionately. "Let's do something together tonight." He peered at Maggie then Wetzel. Before Maggie could respond, Wetzel said, "I dunno, pard. You two deserve your quiet time together." He pursed his lips. "Besides, three's a crowd as they say."

"The hell they say!" Garcia countered. Frowning, he turned to Maggie. "What about you setting Jackie boy up with your friend Juanita?"

Maggie's eyes lit up. "Sure. You betcha. I'm sure she would *love* to go out with him."

Garcia laughed a throaty laugh as he leaned toward Wetzel. "You just be careful of that Juanita. She's one of them hot-blooded Latin women looking for a husband."

Maggie' face blushed red. "*Juan*!"

"I'm just kidding ol' Jack. How 'bout going to the drive-in together? I'll take my car."

Wetzel shifted from one foot to the other. His face was flushed. "Sure, Juan, but I got to do the chores at home first."

"No sweat. I'll go with you after school and help out. I've not seen your mom for awhile." Garcia's face turned serious. "I'm sorry they kicked you off the football team for that whipping you gave Peach. Don't seem fair with him starting the ruckus an' all."

"It's all right, Juan. I had a choice to make, and I made the wrong one by hitting him. I could've left it alone, but I let my temper get the best of me." Wetzel took a deep breath and exhaled. "My mom says everyone makes choices in life and sometimes you suffer the consequences, depending on which road you take. I got no beef coming."

Maggie intervened, "How did the court appearance go with Peach's father filing aggravated assault charges against you?"

"I pled guilty to simple assault. Wasn't much use in denying it didn't take place what with all the witnesses present in the locker room. The judge says I got two choices—either go to jail or join the army. Either way it leaves my mom alone to work the ranch. If I join the army, he'll suspend all jail time in lieu of service to my country and lessen the charge to a misdemeanor."

"But ... but ... Jack. There's a war going on over in Vietnam. People are being killed. You—" Maggie pleaded, her voice trailing off.

Wetzel's somber face reflected his displeasure with the idea as well. Garcia slapped him again on the shoulders saying, "Well, pard. If you're thinking about joining the army, you've got some serious living to do here in Silver City ... starting tonight at the Drive-In with Juanita Flores!"

CHAPTER THREE
Fort Benning, Georgia, 1967

Wetzel filed off the TWA commercial plane with the seven other men from his company. Fort Benning appeared to be a large military base; the red clay soil, pine trees and dark and muddy Chattahoochee River nearby was a nice change from Fort Ord, California, with endless sand hills where he and his company had participated in lengthy marches and drills at the Advanced Infantry Training (AIT) site. He hated Fort Ord with a passion. The instructors told them they would never see the sun shine once there and damned if it wasn't so—he never did for the entire eight weeks. On his meager time off, he traveled to Monterrey or Carmel. At least the sun always shone there!

He'd completed Basic Infantry Training at Fort Leonard Wood, Missouri. Like the rest of the draftees, his hair was shorn and he was subjected to constant yelling and screaming by drill instructors, physical training (PT)—the 40 yard crawl, grenade throwing, running the mile under five minutes in full combat gear including boots, pull ups, and the bars. His attitude and athleticism from high school assisted him in excelling in PT with high scores and being awarded a weekend respite from the dreary, stressful training.

While marching one day on the drill field, he bounced along gaining the attention of the Drill Instructor (DI). The DI walked up alongside him and tapped him on his steel helmet with his stick. "You raised on a farm, boy?" Wetzel had answered the affirmative with the DI grinning and responding, "It figgers. You march like you was walking behind a damned mule and plow."

He learned to take the Korean War vintage M14 rifle apart and put in back together, know all the parts by name, and he became a fair shot. And at AIT he'd learned to use a map and compass and to shoot a 30 caliber machine gun, .45 caliber pistol, and practiced extensive bayonet training.

Once graduation was over, the "old man" or captain of their company singled out seven of the men, Wetzel included, and advised them they'd received great orders, outstanding assignments as Scout Dog Handlers. Wetzel asked what the handlers did and was told they were point men for the infantry. Somehow, he didn't feel as elated as his superior officer. It certainly didn't feel like such a great assignment to him. He felt apprehensive; however, he knew the rest of his company from AIT had orders to report immediately to Vietnam for assigned infantry duties.

The lucky seven were shown their quarters and the head trainer Sergeant First Class Miller took all twenty-six handlers for the platoon down to the kennels where the dogs were kept. Miller was a ramrod straight "lifer". Although smaller in size, he reminded Wetzel of his late father—what he could remember of him. The sergeant wore his baseball cap cocked slightly to the right on his closely cropped graying hair, the brim curled, the fatigue shirt with its rank proudly displayed on the shoulder, and pants pressed and creased to military correctness. The pants were tucked into highly polished black boots.

In a deep, penetrating voice, Sergeant Miller advised the men they should be proud to belong to Infantry Platoon Scout Dog (IPSD) School, and the dogs were to be used for searching out enemy snipers and ambushes, booby traps, but most importantly to save the lives of American infantry soldiers. Each of the handlers was instructed to choose one of the dogs.

Wetzel moved in close to observe the dogs inside the kennel. He stood for a while then squatted on his heels as his quick eyes spied a smaller black and tan with brown eyebrows sitting back on his haunches in the corner watching the wild melee of other dogs barking and snapping at the men advancing toward them. The German Sheppard weighed about fifty pounds. His eyes were red which intrigued Wetzel, but he was more interested in the calm way the dog acted in the midst of such chaos. A soldier approached him; he growled, bared his teeth, and laid his ears back, but he didn't lunge at the man as other dogs were doing. Nervous and most likely not accustomed to animals, the soldier backed up and turned toward another dog nearby. Wetzel retrieved the five foot choke chain and leather leash from the ground, stood and walked directly to the black and tan. The mature dog looked to be about two years old to Wetzel, who had been around stock dogs all his life. *Those red eyes!*

Feeling no fear, Wetzel did not hesitate as he neared the dog and his hazel eyes locked with the red as he and the animal surveyed each other for less than a second. Then Wetzel reached out with the chain and said softly, "Easy, boy. It's just ol' Wetzel." His unflinching hand touched the dog's head, and he slipped the choke chain in place. The growling and bared fangs ceased, but the ears still remained laid back. He saw a name plate titled "Smoky" riveted to the leather collar. These dogs had been owned by others outside the military and donated to the U.S. Air Force. The Air Force had kept the larger dogs and given the rest of the lot to the Army.

Wetzel squatted on his heels directly in front of the dog

that he now claimed as his. He reached forward and with both hands held the shaggy head firmly between them. "Well, Smoky ol' boy, I reckon you an' me ... we're a team from now on ...till death do us part." he said grimly to his new partner. As the dog's eyes remained locked with his new master, his ears stood at attention.

Sergeant First Class Miller had them line up with their prospective dogs. He looked at each of the men, many of whom were trying unsuccessfully to control their dogs. "Listen up! This dog is your companion from here on—that is till your tour in Nam is over—so get to know him. And I mean know him well. It might just save both your lives as well as countless other fellow soldiers. This training will last a total of three months with you and the dog bonding and learning together. During this time, you and *you alone* will take care of your dog, including feeding him each night. You will go through obedience school, teaching your dog basic commands to heel, sit, down, stay, and come. This will be accomplished by verbal means as well as hand signals. Lastly, you will train together to scout for the army.

Gentlemen, your dog's personality will in essence over time become yours. As I've said many times, *feelings always run down the leash*. If you're a lazy son-of-a-bitch, your dog will become the same. However, if you have spirit, likewise he will perform well for you." Sergeant First Class Miller paused, looking again at each of the dog handlers. "Maybe he'll save your life or those of others. It's up to you. And gentlemen, *I* will be watching ... especially for the lazy sons-a-bitches."

CHAPTER FOUR
Central Highlands, South Vietnam, May, 1967

Buck Sergeant E-5 Jack Wetzel stood motionless near his scout dog watching the sun pop out from under the thick clouds. An ivy leaf insignia and three chevrons adorned the shoulder of Wetzel's combat fatigue shirt. The dog had started alerting that morning, getting hot on something, but they couldn't find the enemy. Smoky nudged his leg, and as he looked down at the wet animal, rain dripped from his camouflaged helmet. The ace of spades on the front of the helmet signified the Army's 4th Infantry Division.

Damn monsoon! He cursed silently to himself then said out loud, "Sorry, Mom." When he'd first arrived at Jackson Hole Fire Base in the Central Highlands of Viet Nam in February, it was the latter part of the dry season, and boy was it dry—like a popcorn fart! Since April the weather had consisted of constant light showers then the sun would emerge unexpectedly for a short while only to disappear with the unrelenting rain. He was told this monsoon wet pattern would continue day and night until October when the rain would cease and the dry season cycle begin again. He shifted his weight to his right side and felt the water squish in his wool sock and canvas combat boot. Boots didn't last long as they dry-rotted quickly in the monsoon season. About every other month, he'd swap for two new pairs of boots and acquire some new thick wool socks.

It was hard to work the dog in the rain and dangerous. The scent just wasn't as easily detected in wet weather. Undoubtedly, the scout dogs proved to be valuable assets for the infantry. He knew from training that dogs have the ability to scent forty times better than man, had twenty times better hearing, and ten times better sight. He and Smoky had done well though for the first few months, and the "old man" liked using the team since they discovered a huge cache of weapons and rice the month prior. The "old man" was captain of B Company, Second Brigade of the 4th Infantry Division. The title "old" was an affectionate term and didn't really have true meaning to the nineteen-year-old Wetzel as he knew the captain to be twenty-six and regular army.

Wetzel's tent was situated in the middle of the forward fire camp near the company commander's tent. The "old man" wanted the dog close by. The dog always slept at Wetzel's feet. Wetzel tried to find a place where he could chain Smoky to a tree or heavy bush due to all the foot traffic in camp. Smoky would growl at the soldiers passing by. Many tried to pet him, but he simply did not like it and he snapped at them. Several officers had yelled at Wetzel for his dog scaring the men as they walked by at night, but the "old man" always backed him up by saying, "Dammit, you tell your men to stay the hell away from Jack's dog."

Generally, two scout dog teams from the 50th Platoon would work together in the field. There were 10-12 dog handlers or four to five scout dog teams at the Main Base Camp in Pleiku, and they were alternated back and forth for use in the field at Jackson Hole and Oasis Fire Bases. Spotter planes saw something suspicious, and the company commanders would call for the dogs to assist in searching out and ultimately finding the enemy. Occasionally, the dog teams participated in air assaults for the First Brigade of the 7th Air Cavalry Division, flying in helicopters with the combat troops.

Smoky growled, arousing Wetzel from his thoughts. He slung the adjustable stock M-16 rifle to his shoulder as he saw Weapons Platoon Sergeant Bill Merrell approach. Sergeant Merrell was a 27-year-old army regular who knew combat operations well. Wetzel admired and appreciated working with the professional soldier. Dressed ready for the field, Merrell was a stocky, well-made man; a tough hard man, but affable to those he liked, and he liked Jack Wetzel.

"Howdy, Jack." He pulled a pack of cigarettes from the pocket of his fatigue shirt. He offered the pack to Wetzel, who took one of the Lucky Strikes, lit it with his pocket lighter and lit Merrell's cigarette for him. "You an' Smoky ready to work?"

"We're ready, Bill." Wetzel looked up at the cloudy, rain-filled sky. "I hate working in this damn rain—the dog has so much trouble finding a scent." Tobacco smoke drifted from his nostrils.

Merrell shook his sandy, short-cropped head in agreement, enjoying the smoke. His blue eyes studied the young man beside him. "Why don't you feed your dog, Jack. Let him rest a bit. You've been working hard all morning an' it's close to noon. I'll take my platoon out in a small circle 300 meters or so for a quick looksee. Then we'll come back in and take you and the dog with us for a better surveillance look."

"You sure? Me an' Smoky are ready to go," returned Wetzel.

"Naw. Get some rest. I'll need you later." He slapped Wetzel on the back, turned and was gone.

Twenty minutes passed. Wetzel had finished feeding Smoky and was placing his field gear into his ruck sack—8-

10 canteens of water, c-rations, dog food and the scout harness, poncho and liner. Suddenly, the stillness of the day was broken as heavy fire erupted from the direction Merrell's platoon had gone minutes before. Mortar and rocket fire exploded. Thunderous, earth shattering explosions. The Nine Days in May Battle had begun. Smoky whined as Wetzel stood there momentarily caught off guard. Then he grabbed the leash and he and the dog sprinted for the Company Commander's tent.

From just outside the tent, he heard Sergeant Merrell on the radio calling in air strikes—something about running into a regiment size North Vietnamese force. A short time later, Merrell advised his platoon was cut off from returning to base.

As the afternoon progressed, the situation worsened. Wetzel was assigned to help defend the perimeter with everyone else in B Company. The fire base itself was being pounded by mortar and rocket fire. In the night the North Vietnamese troops began probing and attacking the perimeter.

Wetzel positioned himself near what appeared to be a big Cypress tree back in the States. Smoky lay near his feet. A claymore mine exploded in the distance then another, men screamed, continuous then sporadic shooting. Shots whined over Wetzel's head. He returned fire where he saw muzzle flashes in the dark night from the perimeter. Mass confusion enveloped the camp. It seemed as though everyone in camp was yelling, screaming, or talking on the radios all at once. He felt alone and feared for his life for the first time in the war.

The sky lit up with a loud explosion near him. The thunderous roar split his ear drums and the shock wave threw him violently to the ground. When he came to he couldn't hear anything. He reached frantically for his rifle, found it nearby and had the presence of mind to remove the nearly empty magazine and insert one fully loaded from his ammo pouch. As an afterthought, he reached down, procured the bayonet from its scabbard and snapped it into place on his M-16. *Where's Smoky?* An icy chill ran up his spine as he searched. Unable to hear, he decided to yell for the dog anyway, but still could not find him. Crawling a short distance on his hands and knees, he felt something warm against his hand. It was Smoky! He felt the dog's body with his hands searching for wounds. His hands came away wet. He held them up to his face and smelled blood. The dog stirred against his leg. *He's alive!*

Wetzel looked up just in time to use his rifle to parry a bayonet thrust from an enemy soldier directed at his chest. He came up fast from the ground and drove his own bayonet deep into the North Vietnamese soldier's torso. He slammed his right boot hard against the man's chest and jerked the bayonet free. As the soldier fell, Wetzel shot him. Swallowing hard, unable to breathe, he dropped to his knees again.

Seeing other enemy soldiers approaching, he fired three round bursts into each silhouette racing towards him in the darkness. Rounds whizzed and zipped past him in the dark rain-filled night of terror. He slung the rifle over his shoulder, grabbed the dog as best he could and dragged him back to the large tree.

Upon further inspection, he found the immense tree was hollowed out near the base; barely enough room for him to crawl into. Quickly pulling the injured Smoky in with him onto his lap, he searched for enemy combatants, the unslung rifle held tightly out in front of him. Air Force F-105s swooped in dropping bombs and the artillery from

Jackson Hole Fire Base pounded the enemy further up the mountainside. The ground shook, the night sky lit up intermittently, but Wetzel couldn't hear a thing. His strained eyes ached in dry sockets from searching for the approaching enemy and attempting to determine friend from foe as he sat propped up, hugging the injured scout dog tightly to him. *Our Father who art in heaven*— Silence. *Hallowed be thy name ... please help me.* Ominously, in the inky blackness of the deadly night and unbeknown to man and dog, the shadow of the mountain crept ever so slowly toward the two sitting quietly in the hollowed-out tree.

***

The following day, the North Vietnamese advance was stopped and the enemy retreated into the mountains. Smoky had nonlife-threatening shrapnel wounds. The Americans found Merrell's platoon all dead—with one exception. The North Vietnamese had overrun their position, killing anyone still alive. The lone survivor told of enemy soldiers walking among the dead and dying American soldiers and shooting those still living in the head after stealing all their belongings. That soldier's survival was credited to his ability to play as though he were dead. A North Vietnamese soldier took his clothes, boots, rifle, and then while sitting on his back stole his wedding ring. Somehow, no doubt due to concentrating on the theft, he simply forgot to shoot the American in the head upon receiving orders to withdraw hurriedly from the field.

Wetzel observed the lone survivor. He felt very sad as he peered at the pale, frightened face; his fellow soldier rocking back and forth, moaning to ghosts that would never be forgotten. Would this man forever be a "basket case" due to the harrowing experience?

Suddenly Wetzel realized his hearing had returned!

CHAPTER FIVE
The Battle of Dak To, South Vietnam-November, 1967

It was fall and the dry season had begun the previous month. Wetzel leaned over Smoky, removed the choke chain and leash to replace it with the scout harness. That meant business to Smoky. He urged the dog, "Search, boy ... search ... *hunt 'em up!*"

The point team headed directly into the thick jungle in advance of the infantry company's main body. The green mountains shimmered in the morning sun. Water from the natural, clear mountain springs reflected sunlight as the moving body of water descended from high ridgelines to the valleys below and the awaiting rice paddy fields. Wetzel, his M-16 slung over his shoulder, hung onto the scout harness strap with both hands. He was flanked by his armed body guard and the platoon sergeant immediately behind the dog team with compass in hand to lead the way.

It took all of Wetzel's concentration to watch the scout dog. It was a stressful time for him. He intently watched the dog's nose and ears. At night, he taped white tape on the back of the dog's ears so that he could see the alert movement advising of danger. The wind was blowing directly at them. *Perfect for scenting the enemy!* He hated working his dog with the wind at his flanks narrowing the scent tunnel. A man could get into trouble real quick, and he flatly refused to work the dog with the wind at his back. They moved steadily through the jungle, the platoon sergeant advising the direction of travel. Suddenly, Smoky threw his head up in the air.

"Watch, boy ... watch, boy," encouraged Wetzel, a bad feeling in the pit of his stomach.

If he stops, it'll be a trip wire. Wetzel felt tightness in his shoulders. But the scout dog didn't stop, only slowed his walk, his ears up and pointing forward, nose raised. Wetzel stopped the dog from proceeding farther into the jungle. He turned to the platoon sergeant and whispered, "There's something up there, Sarge ... a sniper ... maybe ... hell, I don't know."

The sergeant nodded and spoke into his radio, then: "The old man says to move back to the ridge behind us. Word is the 66th and 88th North Vietnamese Regiments might be in the area. He'll send in airstrikes to clear the way for us."

Wetzel sat high on the ridge with Smoky at his feet. The dog heard the planes approaching long before he did. They roared over the company's position, all F-105 jet fighters, the Air Force's best. One after the other, he watched them come in low at the position called in and drop their bombs. All morning long he watched strike after strike with fascination as the area was flattened like a pancake. As with the other bombed-out areas, he knew very few animals would survive—maybe a few monkeys if they were lucky. One of their claymore mines at the camp perimeter had killed a tiger once. Blown his belly out.

It was noon. The Air Force had completed their bombing runs. Time to "lock and load" and move up the mountain, find the enemy or whatever was left and destroy them. Wetzel and Smoky along with his body guard, a young redheaded soldier, and the first squad with the platoon sergeant were the first up to the flattened ridge top—about seven or eight of them. The rest of the men were strung out further down the slope coming up behind them. Smoky lay down to rest. The First Lieutenant of the platoon arrived and immediately began giving orders: "You men set up a machine gun over here for covering fire." He pointed to another location along the ridge. "I want –"

Wetzel heard a "pop" much like a cap pistol. The First Lieutenant silently fell to the scorched earth without a sound, a bullet hole in his forehead. *Sniper!* Caught off guard like the rest of the squad, Wetzel hesitated momentarily, and the North Vietnamese, who had been hiding in bunkers, opened fire.

Someone shouted, "Let's get the hell outta here." The American soldiers scrambled down off the hill. Wetzel's body guard dropped his rifle, clutched his chest and fell backward out of the dog handler's sight.

Wetzel felt Smoky at his side, warm against his leg. Raw fear ate at his belly. Bullets pinged overhead and burrowed into the ground nearby, kicking up dust and ashes from the bombing. He resisted the urge to run downhill, turned and ran to the fallen officer. He reached out to grab his fatigue shirt front and felt someone beside him—the platoon sergeant! The sergeant's face was grim, but showed no fear. He helped Wetzel hoist the dead Lieutenant up onto his shoulders then supported him as they both struggled off the hill and down the slope amidst withering enemy fire. Wetzel didn't know why he wasn't killed. He remembered a saying of his mother's: "Just meant to be ... living to do something else worthwhile in this ol' world of ours."

His legs began to falter after fifty yards; he stumbled and would have fallen if the platoon sergeant had not supported him and his heavy load. "Let me take 'im, Jack," he called out in the roar of battle. Wetzel shook his head and somehow forced his body to align with his mind that was already set to get the job done. As they made it to safety, the roar of jets low overhead filled the air. Boom! Loud, thunderous roars, followed by the seared earth shaking, twisting, turning; it was difficult to stand. Wetzel lay next to Smoky. The red eyes beneath tan eye brows did not tell him what the scout dog was thinking.

***

Jets bombed the surrounding area over and over again. Silence replaced the deadly roar, and once again Wetzel found himself trudging back up the same hill he had fled hours before. After attaining the summit of the hill, he searched diligently for his point body guard. He had to dig in the churned up mounds of scorched earth, but he found the dead red-headed soldier who was stripped of his gear, weapons, and clothing except his fatigue trousers. Wetzel covered him with his poncho liner. Enemy soldiers lay on the ground, some half-way out of bunkers that had been hidden prior to the second wave of airstrikes. The Americans soon discovered the bunkers were connected by tunnels that encircled the entire mountain.

Wetzel stood over a dead North Vietnamese soldier. He was struck by how closely the man looked like an American Indian. The long black hair and facial features looked almost Manchurian. The soldier had a brand new uniform and ruck sack containing a new unused razor, AK-47 rifle with the bayonet fixed. On his feet were sandals made of tire tread secured to his feet by straps of inner tubing.

Jack Wetzel drew air deep into his lungs and exhaled slowly. He looked out over the surrounding countryside as far as he could see, beyond the bombed-out, denuded wasteland to the green sun-lit hills and mountains in the far distance. He felt a lump forming in his throat as he thought of home, his mother, and his beloved New Mexico. It all seemed so far away.

CHAPTER SIX
Sydney, Australia- Christmas, 1967

Two weeks R&R! Rest and relaxation, courtesy of the U.S. Army. He stepped out onto the veranda of the White Haven Hotel located on Kings Cross Highway, Sydney, Australia. The wide, blue ocean had no end to it; the yachts, the larger boats carrying goods, the ferries carting people in the harbor was almost as pleasing to his eyes as the blue, sunny skies overhead reminding him of New Mexico and home. He had forgotten about a world worth living in. Ten long, grueling months of war and only two lousy months left then home, by God. He adjusted his new suit and tightened the neck tie, all courtesy of the U.S. Army. *Damn, he felt good!*

The telephone rang in the room. He stepped back inside saw his R&R buddy, Jim Lane, pulling on his trousers near the bed. Lane hailed from Houston, Texas and was assigned to the First Air Cavalry. Wetzel answered the phone. It was Mrs. Dorothy Higgins, their "adopted" mother, who had graciously assisted them during their short stay in Sydney on behalf of the Australian government. Mrs. Higgins was a wonderful sweet lady of 60 years. She reminded Wetzel of Aunt Bea on the "Andy Griffith Show".

"Good-dayee, Jack. How are ye an' Jimmy this fine day?" Mrs. Higgins' voice crackled over the phone line.

"Fine, Mrs. Higgins. Thank you for all you've done for us." Wetzel cradled the heavy phone on his shoulder as he straightened his tie once more while looking in the mirror.

"You Yanks ... don't party so bloody hard that ya don't make the yacht race in the harbor tomorrow morning, ya hear?"

"Yes, ma'am. The sailboat race. What time was that again?'

"Ten o'clock sharp. I'll send a limo over for ya."

"We'll be bright-eyed and bushy tailed, ma'am," Wetzel replied then hung up the phone. He looked to his partner, who had finished dressing and was straightening his tie. Grinning from ear to ear, he said, "Shall we?"

Lane bowed, sweeping his arm toward the door of the hotel room. "After you. I must saay, ol' chap, it's a *cracker* o' a day."

"Too right, mate. A bloody good 'un." Wetzel chuckled at their sad attempts to sound like true Australians.

***

It was late. How late Wetzel had no idea, and furthermore he couldn't care less what time it was. They had taken the cab from the hotel to the nearest pub and immediately asked for two large mugs of beer. Both soldiers downed their respective mugs of beer. Wetzel reached in his back pocket for his billfold to pay for the beers and found it wasn't there. He panicked and couldn't think what to do next. Calming down, he was able to remember the name of the cab company and that the cab was #19. He called and asked the same cab to return to the pub. Luckily, the cab hadn't picked up any other passengers, and Wetzel found the billfold on the floor of the cab next to the door. His airline tickets, shot records, and $300 cash were still inside. He breathed a huge sigh of relief.

Hours passed, beer flowed. A large, raw-boned man entered the pub with two women in tow. They stood for a moment just inside the crowded, noisy establishment looking for a place to sit. The man spied Wetzel and Lane at a table with empty chairs nearby. The trio sauntered over, stopping in front of the two soldiers.

"Good-dayee, mates." The man's round face produced a big smile. "I wonder ... if you would be so kind as to allow us to sit at your table." He looked furtively around the crowded room. "Bloody crowded, ain't it?"

Wetzel stood, although unsteadily. "Sure. No problem, have a seat."

The man guffawed, turned to the two women. "Bloody Yanks 'es what we go 'ere." Both women smiled and sat down next to the soldiers. The man continued to stand. "Me name is Mike, mates, an' these two sheilas are Betty ... me sister, and 'er friend ..." Confusion showed on his rotund face.

The woman sitting next to Lane answered sweetly, "Cora." She licked her red lips as she held out her hand to Jim Lane. "Me name is Cora." She was not quick to remove her hand from his grasp. Mike sat down in an empty chair and ordered a round of beer for everyone.

An hour and several large beers later, Wetzel noticed Mike had disappeared. His sister, Betty, was snuggled up next to him. She placed her arm around his shoulder the other hand on his knee. " Sooo ... Jack," she whispered in his ear, "found any pretty Australian women to run with?" as she nuzzled his ear, her hand firm on his leg.

For the first time during the evening, he noticed her as a woman and appreciated her closeness, her warmth and femininity. He said with a thick tongue, "No, ma'am."

Betty grinned mischievously then as an after thought, she quipped, "Ahh ... an' a polite one, too. You Yanks could teach our Australian men a thing or two."

Wetzel reached over held her by the shoulders and

kissed her softly. For the first time in almost a year, he felt a stirring in his loins.

CHAPTER SEVEN
Jackson Hole Fire Base, Central Highlands South Vietnam, February, 1968

The monsoon season was still a few months away. Not till April, thought Wetzel. *Thank God, I only have a week left to go on my tour of duty, and then adios, amigos.* He'd be the hell outta Nam and on to sunny New Mexico. When he returned from R & R in Australia, it hadn't been the same. His hands shook when out in the field, and he didn't volunteer anymore for others combat duties. He'd tasted and seen there was *real* life out there in the world, and he wanted more than anything to be a part of it now. Lately, he'd been assigned "palace guard", patrolling the perimeter of the fire base with Smoky.

His mother wrote many months ago that things were hard but fine at the ranch. Neighbors were helping her and for him not to worry. She also said his friends Juan Garcia and Maggie O'Brian married right out of high school and were expecting a child. A more recent letter from his mother contained bad news. Juan Garcia had been drafted into the army and was most likely headed for Vietnam.

Wetzel walked to the Company Commander's headquarters in the center of the fire base. Numerous tents covered the sprawling base, with bristling artillery pieces on the south end. He straightened his baseball cap before entering. Passing several clerks busily working on their typewriters, he was allowed to enter the "the old man's" office.

Captain Mossman answered his salute and said, "What

can I do for you today, Jack?" He eyed the mound of paperwork cluttering his desk and in-box.

"Well, sir. It's about Smoky."

Eyebrows raised and genuine concern showed on the officer's face. "Oh, is he hurt or sick?"

"No sir. He's fine." Wetzel bit his lower lip. "I ... uh ... I'd like to take him home with me when I go."

Captain Mossman sighed, leaned back in his chair, and looked directly at the young scout dog handler standing before him. "We've been over this before. The dog belongs to the U.S. Army. They say *no*." He leaned forward in his chair, elbows on the desk. "And I echo their answer, *No, goddammit!*"

"But, sir. He's a one-man dog—answers only to me. Has for sometime now. He'll kill a replacement handler he doesn't know ... or seriously hurt him."

The captain stood. "It's not up to me." He scratched his head as he made direct eye contact with the young soldier. "I don't want to hear anymore about this, Jack. This is the end of it. Do you understand?"

"Yessir." Wetzel dropped his gaze.

"There's another matter." The captain walked around his desk. "I need you and Walters to escort the payroll from Saigon."

"Sir?"

"You heard me. I want your two dog teams ready to go in the morning."

"But ... I've only got a week left, sir. Can't someone else—"

"No. I want you to go. I can depend on *you* to get the job done."

Wetzel hesitated, his heart in his throat.

"That'll be all, soldier."

"Yes, sir," Wetzel said, saluted then left headquarters.

He kicked at the ground outside. *Shit!* A low level helicopter flight 350 miles to Saigon *and back*. Even if they weren't shot down, the awesome responsibility for the company's payroll of ... say seven to nine *million* dollars! *Shit!*

***

They made it to Saigon without any problems. No one even shot at them. The two dog teams sat guarding the payroll all night before they started the return trip. The dogs were muzzled. Wetzel was feeling good about everything. It started raining. Then it began to rain hard, and they were in the middle of a severe thunderstorm. The pilot hollered at a flight crewman to get the dog handler to close his damned door. The crewman tapped Wetzel on the shoulder and pointed at the door.

Wetzel saw the door latch wasn't properly closed on his side of the aircraft. He attempted to secure the door and lost his grip on the wet, slippery handle. The door flew wide open and the storm tore it from its hinges. It was there one moment then gone the next, blown completely clear from the helicopter. Heavy rain poured in on all of them, drenching them to the bone. The pilot yelled something and began to turn the ship around in a fairly tight circle searching for the door.

Within minutes they flew low to the ground almost touching the tall bamboo trees and passed over the mangled door lying on the jungle floor beneath them. The pilot turned to Wetzel and said into the microphone, "Son, take a good *long* look down there. You just cost the U.S. Army $1,500." Nothing else was said to him for the rest of the flight back to base. Everyone was thoroughly drenched and cold. And mad as hell at him for it.

***

Bags were packed and ready to go. Jack Wetzel wore his dress uniform for his return trip back to the United States and home. They would be shipped back via the northern route through Tokyo to Alaska, and on to Fort Lewis, Washington, home to the 4th Infantry Division. His tour of duty in Vietnam was over and service to his country almost complete. He should have been elated. So happy that he'd jump high in the air and kick his heels together. Hell, he should've been laughing out loud, but he wasn't. He was crying like a damn love sick fool. Quietly, he sobbed as his heart ached deep within his breast.

He squatted on his heels as he had done in the beginning, as he had done for months in the field, holding this great friend of his ... this wonderful animal who had saved his life countless times. Tears rolled down his cheeks as he held Smoky tight to him not wanting to let him go. Ever! He breathed in the very essence of his friend and companion so he would never, *ever* forget him.

A loud voice sounded off behind him, "Goddamn it, Wetzel. Hurry it up! Let's get the hell outta this war damn zone."

Wetzel released his grip and leaned back still squatting on his heels. Sad hazel eyes locked with red. He saw the deep understanding of true friendship and unrelenting love in those red eyes just as he had when he'd first met him.

"I'll be seein' ya one day, pal."

CHAPTER EIGHT
Near the Gila National Forest Boundary, New Mexico, Spring 1972

Roger O'Brian stood on the front porch of his old ranch house. His old stock dog had alerted him to the arrival of unlikely guests. He tipped his battered, sweat-stained hat back from his forehead as he watched the green Forest Service truck bounce its way toward him on the rough unmaintained road leading to the ranch house and outbuildings. The dog began to bark loudly and reminded him that the animal didn't take to strangers. In fact, he'd bitten the last visitor. O'Brian laughed softly to himself. Tore the seat right out of his green breeches, by God. The Forest Service son-of-a-bitch deserved it. *Tryin' to reduce the cattle on my allotment!* And him a green behind-the-ears college boy who knew nothin' 'bout ranchin' in the first place.

His Irish temper flared, his cheeks flushed. O'Brian was a big hulk of a man, over six feet tall, barrel-chested, and in his mid-sixties. His old faded Wrangler jeans hung from his narrow bony hips and bowed legs. Outdoor living and the incessant New Mexico sun had burned his face a dark brown and baked deep creases in the leathery skin. *What the hell does the Forest Service want now? The sons-a-bitches never show up unless they want something.* He withdrew a red handkerchief from his back pocket and blew his nose then tucked it in the back pocket with a frayed hole at the bottom.

The green truck bearing U.S. Forest Service insignia on

both door panels came to a halt. The metal door creaked as it opened and a tall young man stepped out. He wore the Forest Service uniform, the tan shirt complete with insignia patch on the right shoulder and an official badge pinned to his shirt front. The slender man moved easily in the faded Wrangler jeans and well-used White's Packer boots. The old man sensed that he knew this man, this intruder who worked for his hated enemy. Leaning forward, he squinted his eyes so as to clearly see the face, but he could only make out a deep shadow beneath the wide-brimmed straw hat the man wore.

As the man neared the porch, the stock dog ceased barking and moved stealthily toward him low to the ground. The man turned his attention to the dog. It wasn't a hurried, fearful move, but he kept the dog from flanking him as he changed course and walked directly at the old dog saying, "What's the matter ol' boy? Don't remember me?"

O'Brian thought *that voice? I know it. Who the hell—*

The man stood over the now uncertain dog. His voice was firm but not harsh, "*Sit!*" The dog hesitated then obeyed as he looked up at the stranger. Reaching out a firm hand, the stranger patted the dog on his head. The old dog's tail wagged and, upon seeing that, the man laughed a soft laugh and squatted down on his heels in front of the old dog. Tilting the straw hat back on his head with this thumb, he turned his gaze to the dazed rancher standing on the porch. "I think ol' Pepper remembers me, Mr. O'Brian."

The old rancher's mouth flew open. *A spittin' image of Tom Wetzel ...only taller*. He tried to speak, swallowed and found the words, "Jack? Jack Wetzel?" He took a tentative step off the porch.

Jack Wetzel stood and stepped forward to shake hands heartily with the old rancher. "I reckon it is, Mr. O'Brian."

The old man was pleased with the firm, sincere handshake.

O'Brian surveyed him from head to toe, smiled and said, "I'll be damned." Shaking his head, he added, "You look just like your daddy, boy. Jest set a mite higher up from the ground is all."

Jack Wetzel's flushed face showed his appreciation for the compliment.

"Tom Wetzel was a good friend, boy. Why, back in them days the Forest Service didn't have nothin' but old time Rangers who done it all in the field. Men like your daddy, Jack. They was all goodun's."

"Thank ya, Mr. O'Brian." Wetzel hooked his thumbs in his jeans pockets.

"How's your mama, son?" queried the sincere old man.

"Fine, sir. Still working hard and enjoying it," said Wetzel.

"Good." O'Brian knew Helen Wetzel for the salt of the earth. They didn't come any better. Then he remembered his long forgotten hospitality. "Would ya like to come in? Set a spell?"

"Porch steps okay?"

"Shore is." The old man moved down a step and sat down heavily as the young man sat next to him. O'Brian reached in his shirt pocket, procured tobacco and paper and started to build a smoke. His knarled, arthritic fingers fumbled with the makings. Tobacco spilled from the curled paper and onto the unpainted porch steps.

Wetzel offered him a store-bought Lucky Strike. O'Brian set his makings on the porch step, accepted the cigarette, and broke off the filter tip. He lit it, drew the smoke deep into his lungs then exhaled slowly. "What brings you out here?" Suspicious gray eyes gazed into the young man's hazel eyes.

Ignoring the question, Wetzel asked one of his own, "How's Maggie, sir?"

The gray eyes softened. "She's doing all right, I reckon ... considerin' everything that's happened. She don't make it out here too much anymore. It too hard a trip for the boy an' gas costs so damned much now-a-days."

Wetzel said nothing. He stuck a cigarette in the corner of his mouth and lit it.

"That goddammed Messican knocked her up then took off for Vietnam. Left her to fend for herself, by God," the old man said vehemently.

Wetzel's voice had an edge to it. "Juan Garcia is my friend just as Maggie is, sir." He tossed his cigarette to the ground and stood, eyes blazing.

"The hell ya say!" The old man was caught off guard. *The boy's got some guts to 'im.*

"Juan loves your daughter—"

"He's dead an' you know it, boy," interposed O'Brian.

"Missing in action ... and he was drafted," corrected Wetzel.

"That was over *two* years ago." The old man motioned for Wetzel to sit again. "Jest calm down. Maybe I was a mite rough on the boy."

Wetzel hesitated then sat.

"Maggie always thought highly of you, Jack." He sighed as he gazed at the silhouette of Granny Mountain in the distant horizon deep within the Gila Wilderness. Pepper found a place to sit next to Wetzel.

Wetzel broke the awkward silence. "The District Ranger wants to cut your allotment numbers in half."

"I know it. Pepper run the Range Con off a few days ago when he come with the good news."

"What are you going to do, Mr. O'Brian?"

"I can't make it if they do that to me. I'm already on a shoe string with cattle prices gone to hell, drier'n all get out, an' no rain in sight."

Wetzel stood and lit another cigarette with his pocket lighter. "Split the difference."

"What?" asked O'Brian incredulously.

"The Forest Service wants to cut half; you want status quo." Wetzel rubbed his tanned jaw as smoke drifted from his nose and mouth. "Range is hurtin', Mr. O'Brian. Country won't sustain your full numbers—not now. Offer to cut a quarter in numbers. Compromise. Then promise to rotate those cattle left however often the Forest wants."

The old man shook his head slowly, chewed on his lower lip; he started laughing. "Hell, the sons-a-bitches might just buy off on it." He frowned, the furrow between his bushy, gray eyebrows deepened. "My fences ain't up in a lot o' places for rotating them cows."

"I'll help you. You just give me a holler when you're ready. Don't have a phone myself, but you can leave a message with the Forest Service office at the Cliff Dwellings." Wetzel started for his truck.

"I got to be going, sir."

O'Brian stood and walked with him. "You're a growed man now, Jack. You call me Roger, uh? I don't take much to that mister stuff anyhow." He stopped near the hood of the hated green Forest Service truck.

Wetzel opened the driver's door. "Please say Hi to Maggie for me." The old man's quick eyes saw no wedding ring.

"Why don't ya ... drop by and tell her yourself, Jack. She'll be glad to see you. Been staying with a *viejita*—a nice little Mexican lady in an apartment over across from the Catholic Church. Her and the boy that is."

Wetzel got in and slammed the door shut. He leaned out the window. "I'll do that, Mr. —er, Roger. See ya." The engine roared to life.

The old man walked around to the driver's side as Wetzel put the truck in reverse. "You tell that District Ranger, I won't deal with anyone but you. They come out here again ... I'll sic Pepper on 'em." For the first time in months, he was smiling from ear to ear as he turned and walked toward the house.

CHAPTER NINE

Ex-Tennessee Wildlife Resources Officer Robert McMurtry guided his twenty-six foot U-haul truck along in the right lane on Interstate 10 a few miles west of Las Cruces, New Mexico. He had taken it slow and easy all the way from Maryville, Tennessee, as he was pulling his old '67 Chevy truck behind the U-haul truck. Everything he owned was in the trailer. It wasn't much by most folk's standards, but then he wasn't most people. He was Bob McMurtry, an old farm boy from the Smoky Mountains. A backwoods boy who sure as hell didn't figger owning material things was very damned important in a man's life.

He hadn't ever gotten along with his old supervisor at Tennessee Wildlife Resources or TWR. Bobby Tate was *the* dumbest sumbitch he'd ever met in his entire life of thirty-five years, and there'd been a passel of fellers who he'd knowed and worked with who weren't exactly the sharpest axes in the tool shed. Tate didn't have the ability to catch a poacher out in the woods if his own life depended on it. But he sure liked to ride rough-shod over his subordinates once he had become the boss.

McMurtry laughed out loud. B*ut then again there ain't nobody who kin catch poachers like me—the Master, by God!* He'd had enough and when a Game Warden job opened up in New Mexico, he'd jumped at the chance. He was to start his job with the New Mexico Game and Fish Department in one week. The Heart Bar Ranch would be his new home and work station. It was located about 80 miles north of

Silver City, New Mexico deep within the Gila National Forest according the map McMurtry had studied.

McMurtry turned off I-10 at Deming, New Mexico onto Highway 180 and headed north toward Silver City. *This dadjimmed country's flatter'n a pancake.* Then he noticed a high mountain peak jutting out against the blue sky lined with light, wispy white clouds. He took a quick look at his map lying in the seat beside him. *Cook's Peak. Huh.* At least they've got some mountains in this here dry, desolate, hot country. He removed his well-worn ball cap with "Tennessee Vols" insignia on the front and ran his coarse stubby fingers through his unruly sandy hair. Replacing the cap, cocking it slightly to the right side, he rubbed his bearded jaw and yawned.

McMurtry stood five feet eleven inches tall with two stocky legs supporting a stout wide torso that was beginning to show a small paunch near his belt line. He wore a faded denim shirt and worn, patched brown overalls with the suspender straps tight against his broad shoulders. Unkempt brown hair covered his head, peeking out from under the cap; a brown beard displaying some gray adorned his square face. Bright blue eyes studied the road ahead.

Reaching over to the dash, he picked up the opened cigarette packet, shook one out and stuck it in the corner of his mouth. After lighting it, he rolled the window down about halfway. The cool spring air felt good on his face. He thought he'd like this dadjimmed weather.

He turned off Highway 180 onto 61 and soon noted the Mimbres River running adjacent to the highway. *Members River, huh?* There was no visible water in the very dry river bed. The typical desert vegetation had given way to flat grasslands. He saw a sign indicating the turnoff for City of Rocks State Park. Stopping at the junction of Highway

61 and 35, he saw where Highway 152 headed east to the small village of San Lorenzo and then on through the Black Range, a huge mountain range in the Gila National Forest. He looked briefly at the map and saw Hillsboro Peak was 10,011 feet in elevation. *I'll be dogged. These New Mexico Mountains make the Smoky Mountains look like dadjimmed ant hills.*

McMurtry enjoyed the drive with the highway traversing along the Mimbres River. He felt more at home in the tall pine trees, and when he spotted the sawmill operation on the east side of Highway 35, he was elated. Continuing on north from where the highway veered west away from the river and the U.S. Forest Service Mimbres Ranger Station, the country rose in elevation and its scenery became even more enticing to the old country boy.

Easing the U-haul truck and its extra load around a curve in the road, he spied a beautiful little lake into which fed Sapillo Creek. Lake Roberts the sign advised. He pulled the U-haul truck and towed pickup into the gravel parking lot of a store. The small store was built of stained rough wood and sported a board sidewalk in front of a tall storefront with upstairs windows overlooking the parking lot. His belly growled. For a man who always ate more often and a lot more than he should've, he'd forgotten to eat.

Locking up the truck, he stretched his stocky frame, hitched up his overalls, and walked up the wooden steps and into the country store. A bell jingled merrily as the door opened and closed. An elderly couple stood in the trinkets area and the remainder of the store appeared empty. McMurtry sauntered over to the counter, his soft-bottomed lace-up hunting boots making very little noise. He wondered where the clerk was when he saw a woman bent over behind the counter retrieving a box from a storage cabinet.

The woman wore faded jeans that fit snuggly around her shapely hips and a red and white checkered cotton blouse tucked into the jeans. Enjoying the view from behind more than he should have, McMurtry blushed and looked off at the elderly couple when the woman straightened from behind the counter.

"*Valgamé*," she gasped and covered her mouth with a hand. McMurtry could see that she was tall for a woman, maybe five feet seven inches. *Tall and shapely,* he thought and again his face blushed. Her shoulder length black hair hung loosely about her oval brown face. Then his attention was riveted to her smiling pretty brown eyes that glowed.

"*Lo siento mucho, señor*. I deedn't hear you come up." She placed her small hands on the counter. Discretely, he checked to see she didn't wear a wedding ring. "How may I help you, *señor*?"

He rubbed his scruffy beard with his left hand. "I've got me a powerful hunger, ma'am. What ya got fer vittles?"

The pretty eyebrows knitted. "Veetles?"

He laughed. "You know, ma'am, food. I've not et fer a spell."

She stood and peered at him, taking him all in—the clothes, scruffy appearance, and the dialect.

McMurtry tried to break the awkward silence. "If ya don't mind my asking, ma'am. Jest what exactly are you anyways ... an Injun?"

The woman's brown eyes gazed into the blue eyes of the Game Warden. She smiled and said, "I'm Hispanic, *señor*." She saw the blank look on his face. "Mexican descent."

His face lit up. "Oh ... yeah. I plumb forgot where I was, I reckon."

"And you, *señor*? Exactly, what are you?" The brown eyes were laughing.

"Lil' ol' me?" he quipped as he removed the ball cap and scratched his unruly hair that stuck out in too many places. "Why, I reckon I'm jest a good ol' country boy from the mountains o' Tennessee." He perched the ball cap back on his thick head, cocking it to the right side.

"We don't get too many ... like you ... around thees here parts," she teased.

Laughing at himself, he said, "I reckon not, ma'am." He gathered the courage to ask, "What's your name, ma'am? If'n you don't mind my askin'?"

"I don't mind, *señor. Me llamo, Juanita. ¿Y usted?*"

McMurtry's face frowned. "I'm sorry, ma'am. I don't understand Mexican talk."

"Call me Juanita. What ees your name?"

Tucking his hands in his patched overalls, he replied, "Robert McMurtry. All my friends call me Mac, and if ya don't mind, just leave off that signor title."

The smile returned to the eyes and mouth. The woman seemed to be enjoying the conversation. "Of course. But I think I weel call you ... *Roberto*. Do you mind?"

"If you kin get me some hot vittles shortly so's I can et, you can call me jest 'bout anything that pleases ya, ma'am."

She laughed a throaty laugh that was pleasant to him. If everyone was a nice and friendly as this lady, he was going to like this country. He looked into those pretty brown eyes once more and felt the warmth of genuine friendship. Pursing his lips, he said, "Thank ya, Juanita."

She's smilin' at me agin. Wel-l-l now.

"You're welcome, *Roberto*."

McMurtry had no idea of the meal that awaited him. He ate heartily of the *huevos rancheros* and them green thangs Juanita said were green chilis from Hatch, New Mexico. The very *best* chile in the world, she told him as she offered him a second helping then a third. As he finished eating his new-found meal with several extra helpings of chile, he thought *I'm beginnin' to like this dadjimmed New Mexico.*

Having made a new friend and with his belly full, McMurtry turned onto the Clinton P. Anderson Highway toward the Gila Cliff Dwellings and the Heart Bar Ranch. He drove several miles on the winding road that ran adjacent to Copperas Creek. His belly made deep rumbling sounds. As he saw the header canyon come down off Copperas Peak to his left, he felt a sharp twang in his gut. He wheeled into the parking area called Copperas Vista and barely had enough time to grab the toilet paper from the glove box, jump over the rock vista wall and scramble down the slope into the cover of a piñon pine tree.

You ol' gal, Juanita. He grinned, his blue eyes smiling. *You knowed that there chili was goin' to fix ol' Mac, now didn't ya?*

CHAPTER TEN

Wetzel parked his 1951 Chevy truck in the parking lot behind the Gila Cliff Dwellings Visitor Center. He slammed the door as he exited and said softly, "Stay, Montie," to the young Border collie leaning over the side, wagging his tail. The summer day was warming, and he needed to get on the trail soon. His horse was saddled and ready and his packed gear and food for ten days was waiting for him at the Forest Service barn just down the hill from the Visitor Center. But first, he needed to speak with the District Ranger, his boss.

The Gila Cliff Dwellings administrative site was located deep within the Gila National Forest about 80 miles north of Silver City, New Mexico. The highway and associated administrative buildings, residences, fire helispot and crew quarters had all been completed in 1968. The Gila Wilderness, designated as such in 1924, was the very first designated wilderness in the United States. Folks were right proud of the fact and even more proud that Senator Clinton P. Anderson had arranged for federal funding to provide adequate year around access into the area as well as funding for building the administrative site.

The U.S. Forest Service and the National Park Service shared joint responsibility for administering the site with a Park Superintendent who oversaw the pre-historic Cliff Dwellings and the Visitor Center. A District Ranger was responsible for managing the forest wilderness area itself. It wasn't a difficult task for the Wilderness District Ranger as there were no timber operations allowed within the wilderness. This reduced the stress and work load, but recreation, range, and of course fire suppression duties kept the new Ranger more than busy.

Wetzel removed his Stetson as he entered the back office complex behind the Visitor Center. He wore the tan uniform shirt with the badge over his left pocket and the shoulder emblem designating he worked for the U.S. Forest Service, Department of Agriculture. Over the larger emblem patch was displayed a smaller half-moon emblem, "Gila National Forest". He passed several fire helitack crewmen gathered near the coffee pot in the break room.

One of the men called out to him, "Hey, *guero*. Why don't you come with us to Millie's tonight?" Fernando Cortez grinned broadly displaying even, white teeth beneath his trimmed black mustache. A short, stocky Hispanic in his early twenties, he, too, had served time in Vietnam. Cortez worked directly for Wetzel and was in charge of the helitack crew consisting of thirty-eight seasonal firefighters stationed in quarters at Gila Center. These men were flown by helicopter deep into the wilderness to suppress wildfires caused by lightning and misbehaving humans. Cortez removed his fire hard hat and placed it next to his coffee cup; he filled the worn cup with hot, scalding coffee.

"Naw. I reckon not, Fernando." Wetzel's face broke into a grin. "I'm headed for White Creek today. Besides it's too much money for them ol' ladies."

Cortez's face registered a change from solemn smirk to one of surprise. "*¿Codo duro?*"

Wetzel laughed out loud. "You still want to keep my dog, Montie, for a few days? And I'm not being cheap, just honest!"

"*Sí*, Jack." Cortez slurped the hot coffee.

As Wetzel continued down the hall to District Ranger

Bill Hood's office, he said over his shoulder, "He's out back in the truck. Best take him now; if he gets down to the corrals, he'll want to go with me."

Wetzel shook his head as he thought of Millie's brothel located on Hudson Street in Silver City. Millie had been established there for as long as he could remember. Word was the town fathers had suddenly gotten religion or maybe a conscience. They were finally going to throw her out and shut the lucrative business down. Cortez had referenced in Spanish that Wetzel was too cheap to spend his money there, knowing fully well Jack Wetzel had never been inside the establishment.

He stopped at the entrance to Hood's office. Bill Hood looked up over thick glasses set low on his large, bulbous red nose. His close-cut crew haircut made his large head seem even larger, the ears small in comparison. He quickly looked down and shuffled papers on his desk, and did not speak or indicate for Wetzel to enter the inner sanctum of his small, cramped office. Wetzel stepped into the office uninvited, hat in hand.

"Bill, I need to speak with you, if you have a moment."

District Ranger Hood snorted and threw his glasses on the desk in disgust. He leaned back in his plush chair and said impatiently, "What d'you want, Jack? Can't you see I'm busy? I thought you were headed for White Creek. A bit late, aren't you?"

"Yessir. But my two mules are missing. D'you know where they are?"

Hood leaned forward in his chair, his elbows on the desk, eyebrows arched. "D'you think I don't know? I'm stupid?" He didn't wait for an answer. "Of course I know where they are; I traded them to the Beaverhead District."

Wetzel clutched his hat tightly, careful not to raise his

voice. "What on earth for, sir?"

"The new mules will be cheaper to feed and care for ... that's why," Hood said emphatically.

"But ... sir. There are two small burros down there in the corral. They're not mules. Hell, they're even little for burros. I can't—"

District Ranger Hood stood suddenly. "Don't you sass me, Wetzel! I'm in charge here, and I made a great trade deal with those *mules*." He turned away toward the window which was directly behind the desk. With his hands on his hips he blurted out, "You don't like it, get yourself another job."

Wetzel's eyes narrowed. He took a deep breath before responding, "They'll be fine, sir." He turned to go.

"Good. I'm glad we understand each other." Hood turned from the window. "You ought to know how to take orders without question." His voice was slightly conciliatory. "They tell me you're a frigging war hero. Bronze Star and all that rot."

Wetzel said nothing.

District Ranger Hood placed his hands behind his back, his belly protruding over his belt. "I hired you as General District Assistant because you were a ten-point vet." Hood snorted. "And I've *never* supported that war."

Wetzel would not be provoked.

Sensing an upper hand, District Ranger Hood grinned broadly. "You take good care of my new mules. Ya hear, Jack?"

Placing his Stetson on his head, Wetzel said, "Yes sir." He strode out of the office.

Back in the parking lot he slammed his truck door closed. Wetzel was reminded of the alleged story of his predecessor. Supposedly, when his predecessor had worked for

Hood a mere few months ago, he had needed assistance in filling out a fire report. He went to District Ranger Hood and asked for help, to which he was told angrily, "Hell, I haven't time for you. Go look it up in the goddamned manual." Of course, Hood was referring to the huge assortment of manuals the U.S. Forest Service kept for reference on a plethora of management topics from fire to range and recreation issues, just to name a few.

Anyhow, the man somehow figured out how to complete the report, no thanks to his boss. Several months later, he and District Ranger Hood were saddling up at the barn below the Visitor Center and Hood, being a novice rider at best, had mounted a black gelding appropriately called Midnight. Midnight, overly anxious for a field outing, had swung around swiftly as Hood swung on board upright, and he damned near fell off the other side of the big horse. Well, sensing a poor rider and no doubt feeling his oats, Midnight tossed his bit into the air and took off down the West Fork of the Gila River with District Ranger Hood hanging on as if his life depended on it—which it did.

He shouted to the then General District Assistant, "What do I do, Roy? *Help!*" As his glasses fell from his large bulbous nose, he screamed again, "*What do I do?*"

Well, ol' Roy, having had his fill of District Ranger Hood, just stood there watching his boss disappear behind a thick clump of rabbit brush along the river bed. He shook his head slowly then said quietly, "If'n I was you, Bill, I reckon I'd go look it up in the goddamned manual." Then Roy walked up to the office and turned in his time.

***

Jack Wetzel rubbed his square jaw as he stood inside the corral. He held a nylon halter with a long lead rope attached. As he gazed at the small jenny burro, who stood in the enclosure gazing back at him, all the pent-up anger left him. Short and pot-bellied, her tail and long wooly ears swished at flies. Her dark, large eyes were soft, eyelids fluttering as she stood casually surveying him. As he walked directly toward her, she abruptly turned away, trotted to the furthest corner of the corral and lithely turned her butt toward him, ready to kick when approached. He laughed out loud, hesitated and quickly stepped to the side toward her shoulder while tossing the long lead rope over the top of her neck. Tricked into believing that she was roped, she immediately ceased all defensive activity. He moved in close to her neck and secured the halter.

"My God, lil' gal ... you're not any bigger'n a pound o' soap, are ya?"

She looked up at her captor with those sad, soft eyes. The eyelids fluttered. He grinned, "I think I'm gonna like you. I'll call you ... lemme see ... *Rosita*." As he tied her to the corral post, he thought, *maybe I can leave some of the gear? I don't think you can handle even a hundred pounds, kid.* He felt something tug at his back, and turning, he saw the other burro standing close to him.

The jack burro was a few pounds heavier than *Rosita*, but not by much. His hair coat was a light gray with a white underbelly; a dark hair line ran down the center of his back from the withers and two lateral dark lines proceeded halfway down his shoulders. The burro raised his head, pulled his lips back away from his teeth and brayed loudly. Wetzel couldn't help being amused at the sight. His brow furrowed as he slipped a halter on, thinking of an adequate name for the second burro. He led him over and tied him adjacent to the jenny, *Rosita*.

Then it came to him. *Chochi!* Spanish for Georgie would be perfect for this little character.

As he placed blankets, sawbuck pack saddles, and panniers on the two burros, he was reminded of his father's tales of old Ben Lilly. The legendary mountain man had hunted lion and bear in and around the headwaters of the Gila River for many years. Claiming to have killed 426 mountain lions and 210 bears from 1914 to 1925, he lived in the wilderness with his hunting dogs ... and his burros. Heck, if ol' Ben Lilly had used burros, Wetzel reckoned he could do the same and be damned proud to at that.

CHAPTER ELEVEN

Wetzel touched his spurs lightly to the bay gelding as he rode along the West Fork of the Gila River and passed the trail junction for Little Creek and Little Turkey Park to the west of Brushy Mountain. The alligator juniper and piñon pine trees provided some shade from the heat of the mid-day sun. There were no clouds visible in a blue sky. The two fully loaded burros followed passively along behind the bay; *Chochi* in the lead with *Rosita* in tow, trotting hard to keep up. A small dust cloud followed their movement along the beaten and weathered Forest Service trail.

Jack's father, Tom Wetzel, had been District Ranger for the Mimbres Ranger District in the 1950s. He'd been assisting to suppress a large project fire, the Little Creek Fire, in 1955 when he was unexpectently killed leaving a designated safety zone to go back into the raging wildfire to find a missing firefighter. Jack had never really gotten to know his father as well as he would've liked. He was barely eight years old when his father perished in the fire along with the firefighter he was trying to pack out on his back.

Continuing up the West Fork for another five miles, Wetzel found the heavily loaded burros began to pull back, and he had to dally the lead rope around his saddle horn so he could keep moving forward at a decent pace. He still had a long way to go to White Creek Cabin. A rattlesnake buzzed at him nearby from beneath a rock a ways from the running water. The horse's metal shoes clanged against rocks as the horse and burros splashed through the water at one of hundreds of crossings in the trail up the West Fork from Gila Center. Large rock pinnacles spiraled up into the air, towering over them on either side of the tall canyon walls. Ponderosa pines provided respite from the sun as Wetzel zigzagged around the numerous deadfalls in the trail. *The trail crew's got their work cut out for them this year.*

He came to where the West Fork turned back sharply south and knew the trio was almost to the confluence of White Rocks Canyon and the West Fork. He could smell wood smoke in the air. Suddenly, a man in camouflage appeared on his right, spooking the burros. They bolted behind him and his bay horse reared, almost unseating him. Wetzel whirled his mount to the right and regained control of his horse and the pack stock. He looked again for the sudden intruder and found him leaning against a large Ponderosa pine, his arms folded across his chest. Dressed fully in camouflage shirt and pants, the stocky man grinned as he shouted, "Howdy there, neighbor!"

He dropped his arms to his sides and strode toward Wetzel, who noted the leather shoulder holster underneath his left armpit encasing a .357 revolver, the lace-up hunting boots, the hatless scruffy brown hair and beard. Wetzel gazed into wide, bright blue eyes set on a square face of a solid-built man in his mid-thirties.

"Mister, you damned near caused me a wreck with these pack animals," Wetzel barked.

The man stopped near the bay's shoulder. He appraised both burros carefully, taking his time. "You kin handle these lil' 'uns well 'nough." He guffawed loudly. "Hell, they ain't any bigger'n a minute, are they?"

"They're more'n big enough to get the job done all right," Wetzel interposed hotly.

"Why, back in Tennessee, we'd toss these lil''uns back

in."

The hunter took a step back, looked thoughtfully up at the hardened face of the young horseman. "Don't get all dadjimmed white-eyed on me, son." He pursed his lips while trying to suppress a smile on his face. The blue eyes were already smiling.

Wetzel's eyes narrowed. "Don't get ... *what?*"

"Why, you know—all lathered up—hot under the collar."

"I'm not," insisted Wetzel with a somewhat more conciliatory tone of voice.

"We-l-l-l ... I'm sure proud you ain't. I was fixin' to introduce myself."

Wetzel said nothing as the hunter extended his hand. "The name's Bob McMurtry. My friends call me Mac." They shook hands. "I'm the new Wildlife Officer stationed at the Heart Bar."

"Mr. McMurty—"

"I'd take it as a personal favor if you'd call me Mac."

Wetzel grinned, flicking the reins in his hand. "Pleased to meet ya ... Mac. I'm Wetzel."

The hunter scratched his scruffy brown beard then his thick, unruly hair. "You Jack Wetzel, the Ranger that works outta Gila Center?"

"I am. Though my title's not Ranger."

"You look like a sure 'nough Ranger to me, Jack." McMurtry pointed toward the badge and uniform. Wetzel didn't argue. The Wildlife Officer placed his hands in his pants' pockets.

"You got any law enforcement authority, Ranger Wetzel?"

Wetzel's brow furrowed. "Yeah. Why?"

McMurtry turned on his heel and headed down the

trail. "Come on, I'll show you."

***

As he trailed along behind the stocky Wildlife Officer with the burros in tow Wetzel saw four individuals, two played in the water and the others lay or sat along the bank of the West Fork on the north side across from White Rocks Canyon. Several tents were erected, displaying blue and red colors in contrast to the green river bank. Everyone stared at the approaching Wildlife Officer and the Ranger on horseback. They were all naked and appeared to Wetzel to be in their early twenties; two men and two women and none appeared embarrassed to be caught in their natural state of being!

McMurtry walked up to the nearest man standing in the creek. Waving his arm to the others, he hollered, "All you dadjimmed hippies ... gather round here. We need to talk to y'all."

As Wetzel rode up alongside the skinny naked man standing in the creek, he saw the angry expression on the man's bearded face. Stifling his laugh by dropping his head and letting his hat brim shade the same in his eyes, he said quickly, "Mac, I'll handle this—"

But it was too late, the man exploded in a high pitched screech directed at McMurtry. "You ... you *Gestapo*!" He moved in close to McMurtry, body parts flopping about, and shouted, "How *dare* you order us around!"

McMurtry looked hurt. "Well now, don't go gettin' all white-eyed on me. Y'all look like hippees. You've sure 'nough got long hair." He motioned toward the others. "And all o' ya are standing here on public property all necked an' sech."

"Mac!" Wetzel interjected. "I said I'll handle it."

"Why sure, Jack. You bet." His eyebrows arched, the

face feigning apologies but only hiding the jest of the whole incident. "I'll ... uh ... jist round up these here other hippies so's you kin talk to 'em all at once."

The skinny man standing in the river flung his long wet, stringy hair back from his bearded face and screamed, "*Nooo!*" His pale face transitioned to red, his eyes blazed anger. "You goddamned Smoky Pig *sons-a-bitches!*"

He ran around behind Wetzel to get on the south side, screaming profanities as he went. He slipped on the wet rocks in the river bed, almost fell headlong into the water then recovered as he stood directly behind Rosita. Her head turned and she peered back at him as though he should've known better than to be at that location and range. Her long wooly ears twitched, the soft eyelids fluttered as she kicked straight out behind with both back feet. A sharp, hard kick, legs fully extended, that landed between the man's legs. He let out a blood curdling scream as he fell back, splashing water high in the air. Both burros spooked. It took all Wetzel could do to regain control of them and pull them with him over to the north side away from flailing skinny man.

McMurtry approached the injured "hippee" as the man stood unsteadily on his legs, the cold water rushing past his pale, white body. "Y'all all right?" he drawled.

The man grasped his private parts tightly with both hands. He swayed forward then back as he stood hunched over moaning loudly. McMurtry leaned in to take a closer look, resting his hands on his knees. Shaking his head, he frowned. "Took the hide ... plumb off, I'd say." He whistled low as he took another look and spit to the side. "Best git y'all o'er on the bank yonder and lay down. Come morning you're goin' to be in a world of hurt there, feller."

Wetzel tied his horse and burros a short distance from

the group, who were all gathered around the injured man offering suggestions. The man refused to allow any first aid to his damaged parts. Wetzel succeeded in getting the others to clothe themselves after advising them that family groups with children routinely traveled along the main trail of the West Fork. Then he observed a small plastic bag of marijuana hanging partially out of one of the men's pants pocket. He confiscated the marijuana, obtained identification from the man and wrote him a citation for possession of less than an ounce of marijuana. Wetzel asked a final time if he could assist the injured man and was blatantly refused.

As he walked back to his horse and placed the citation booklet in the saddle bags, he could not help but hear the swearing and cursing from the group intended for his ears. He was reminded of a similar incident when he first returned from Vietnam. In dress uniform at the bus stop in El Paso, he was approached by several individuals with long hair. They called him "baby killer" among other things, spat on him, and chanted anti-war slogans in his face. Remembering his past negative experiences when he had resorted to violence, he didn't hit any of them even though he'd wanted to in the worst way. He had thought, *most likely ignorant and misinformed. Hell, he hadn't asked to go over to Nam in the first place.*

McMurtry appeared as Wetzel mounted the bay and trotted the horse over to where the burros were tied. As Wetzel secured the lead rope for *Chochi*, McMurtry said, "I'm sure proud you had the opportunity to meet me, Jack Wetzel." He smiled broadly. Bright blue eyes smiled.

"Likewise ... Mac." Wetzel tucked a store bought Lucky Strike cigarette in the corner of his mouth and lit it with his silver lighter. The swearing and cursing continued unabated. He offered McMurtry a cigarette.

The Wildlife Officer shook his head and shouted, "*Y'all, shut the hell up!* If I hafta come o'er yonder, I'll throw the whole dadjimmed lot o' ya in jail." The afternoon quiet returned to the West Fork.

"I heerd you was a good tracker, Jack."

Wetzel returned the lighter to his shirt pocket and reached for the lead rope around the saddle horn. "Fair to middlin', I reckon," he said as smoke drifted lazily from his nose and mouth.

"I ain't too shabby myself. Maybe we'll track together sometime."

Wetzel grinned at McMurtry. "Maybeso." He swung the horse around and headed upstream toward White Creek. He was beginning to like this straight forward man from Tennessee.

CHAPTER TWELVE

Several miles further upstream, Wetzel and his burros passed Nat Straw Canyon at the confluence of the West Fork of the Gila River. He was reminded of the Gila Mountain man, Robert Nelson "Nat" Straw, who arrived in the Gila Mountains in the 1880s and lived the rest of his life trapping grizzly bears, lions, and wolves in the wild country. Unlike Ben Lily, Straw didn't use hounds to hunt them, only the dangerous, heavy forty-two pound steel traps. By the 1930s, the grizzlies and wolves had vanished from New Mexico and "Nat" Straw had retired to a small farm near Cliff, New Mexico, to spin tales about his adventurous life in a unique wilderness he had come to love.

Old mountain men and grizzly bears filled Wetzel's mind as he traversed the steep, rocky trail above a deep pool of water just a mile or so down the West Fork from White Creek Cabin. The golden sun had set the sky on fire and cool air had begun to flow down into the canyon bottom as Wetzel rode up to the barn and corrals at White Creek. As he rode by, he saw the horse and pack mules belonging to Jim Hawkins, one of his Wilderness Patrolmen, standing in the corral, their tails swishing at flies. Wetzel rode up to the green exterior door of the cabin leading directly to the kitchen. He ground-tied his bay horse near the door, tied the lead rope for his burros to the saddle horn with a slip knot, and untied the diamond hitch on *Chochi's* pack. After removing the aluminum food panniers from the sawbuck pack saddle, he carried them inside to the kitchen. Hawkins hollered hello at him from upstairs as Wetzel started outside to get his bedroll and clothes bag.

The White Creek Ranger Station had been built for the U.S. Forest Service by the Civilian Conservation Corps (CCC) in the 1930s. The well-built log house or Ranger quarters was nestled in the northwest end of Pine Flat at the confluence of White Creek and the West Fork of the Gila River. Unseen from the cabin site due to its location down in the river bottom, the Jerky Mountains with its dominant peak, Lily Mountain, were due north of the cabin about four miles as the crow flies, with Mogollon Baldy towering due west at 10, 788 feet in elevation about nine air miles away.

The two-story White Creek cabin included a kitchen replete with a large wood cook stove and pantry, a living room with a stone fireplace, and strong wooden stairs leading upstairs to several bedrooms. A handmade wooden rocking chair painted an ugly yellow sat in the living room near the fireplace. A single metal bed had been placed in the dining room near the window that faced south toward the barn and corrals. Wetzel tossed his bedroll and canvas bag containing his clothes and toiletries on the bed. He'd sleep downstairs this time around. Military-style metal bunk beds were arranged in the master and upstairs bedrooms with mattresses rolled atop the metal bed springs.

The sturdy log barn and corrals were located on the south end of Pine Flat about one hundred yards across a broad meadow from the residence. Wetzel walked the distance leading his bay horse and the two burros. The evening shadows were reaching out tentatively to the meadow from the canyon walls. The sun had already set to the west high on the ridge overlooking the Ranger cabin. A slight breeze teased the fringes on Wetzel's riding chaps as he walked along, his spurs clinking occasionally on rocks as he strode near a beaver pond. He tipped back his Stetson with his thumb. *God, I love this country. I'm so blessed to work here.* Suddenly without warning *Chochi* brayed loudly behind him with *Rosita* following suit. Startled, Wetzel turned quickly to look behind him. Then he laughed out loud, a throaty laugh that could be heard clear across the meadow. Also startled by *Choci's* warning, a white-tailed deer readying to feed on the lush green grass of Pine Flat hesitated behind the cover of thick conifer growth.

Wetzel unsaddled the horse and burros, placing the saddles, pack gear, and grain and pellets inside the barn. He took time to walk each animal over to the West Fork, allowed them to quench their thirst in the cold running water then turned them into the corral adjacent to Hawkins' animals. After they had rolled and shook to their satisfaction, he placed canvas *morals* or feed bags containing pellets and grain on each animal. He watched them toss the bags and eat hungrily as ominous canyon walls loomed above dark and craggy.

Later, as he and Hawkins ate supper, a full moon began to light up the landscape outside the log cabin. Hawkins slid his chair back from the table and patted his belly. "That sure was a fine supper, Jack. Them biscuits you made was an extra treat."

Wetzel yawned. "Not too shabby at that, huh?"

Hawkins leaned forward, a serious look on his face. "A damned bear broke into the kitchen some time back. The door was busted and ajar when I arrived yesterday."

"Really?"

"Yep. Hope he don't come back soon expecting more goodies like he raided from the pantry."

Wetzel stood. "Not too likely, Jim." He yawned again as he took the dishes over to the sink to wash them.

"I'll do the dishes," Hawkins said as he stood. "You cooked supper. By the way, you'd best move that damned kindling bucket near your bunk bed to the living room before you trip over it tonight in the dark."

Wetzel didn't respond, but stood looking down at his feet. He had removed his heavy Packer boots earlier and noticed both his big toes were protruding from his socks.

Hawkins looked at his feet and chuckled. "Jeez, Jack, you need to get married and have them holey socks repaired."

Wetzel grinned. "Maybeso."

It was late when Wetzel awakened in the night. The moonlight poured into the living room through the dust-covered panes of the window near the bed. He sat up, listened intently as he heard the horses and burros milling about in the corrals below the house. The horses nickered loudly and the burros brayed out into the still night. *What the hell?* He knew from past experience not to ignore what his animals told him. A good horse always knew way before a man had any idea if something was amiss. He sighed deeply as he thought of his old scout dog Smoky. That dog *always* knew when all hell was ready to break loose. He'd been infallible during the war.

Wetzel stood near the metal cot, listened to the night sounds, but couldn't discern anything that seemed out of order. He wriggled his toes protruding through the holes in his socks and straightened his frame. His white, long-handled underwear made him appear as a ghost in the darkened interior of the cabin. Yawning, he scratched his buttocks near the buttoned trap door in the back. He sauntered over to the opened window, careful to walk around the kindling bucket in the floor, and leaned out the window peering at the corrals a hundred yards distant to the south. The cool night air brushed against his tanned cheek and rustled his thick, disheveled brown hair. The horses, burros, and mules were running back and forth in the corrals, whinnying and braying. *Wish ol' Montie was here.* Wetzel's mind cleared somewhat from sleep as he placed his hands on the window sill to take a better look outside at the commotion.

Suddenly, his view was obscured. He felt a searing, hot breath directly in his face then a loud roar that bellowed out in the night instantly breaking the still silence and deafening his ear drums. He saw the huge, shaggy face, the gaping mouth with large, menacing teeth inches from his face!

Wetzel had thought many times over the years of what he would do if a bear attacked him, but he just stood there, his mouth open his feet frozen to the floor. The roar, again, this time much louder. His ears rang; the hair on the back of his neck stood up, and he had a bad feeling in the pit of his stomach. Raw fear!

Spittle flew into his face, and Wetzel broke and ran from the window. He heard the bear come through the window behind him as he turned to run and its heavy weight hit the floor. He slipped in his loose stocking feet losing traction and tripped over the kindling bucket directly in his path. As he went down, he felt the bear swipe at him, clawing his back side with one of its paws.

The buttons on the trap door of his long johns in the back burst and Wetzel cringed, clenching his teeth as he felt the sharp claws cut into his buttocks. He literally dove under the metal bed with the bear right behind him.

Unable to get under the bed, the bear roared as he stood

on his back feet in the moonlit room. He landed heavily on the metal bed as Wetzel curled into a tight ball beneath it. Wetzel felt the bear reach around and under the side of the bed with one of its paws, as if searching for its prey. The weight of the bed and bear on top of him made it difficult for Wetzel to breathe. His heart pounded in his ears. Another loud frustrated roar from the bear. All Wetzel could think of was why in the hell the damned Forest Service didn't allow them to carry firearms in the wilderness.

A loud BOOM! Then the bear's weight was no longer on the bed and Wetzel was again able to breathe. Another boom, its sound reverberating in the small confines of the cabin, and he knew it was a firearm that had been discharged at close range. He could hear the bear's clawed feet scrambling on the floor then the sound of the large body going through the window.

"Son-of-a-bitch!" exclaimed Jim Hawkins.

The breathless Wetzel gingerly crawled out from beneath the metal bunk bed. Hawkins lit the lantern. As the room was enveloped in light from the Coleman lantern, Wetzel felt himself to ensure all body parts were intact. His eyes quickly assessed the room, the upturned kindling box, the rumpled bedroll and mattress, the blood on the floor and window sill. He turned to Hawkins, who stood staring at him, eyes wide with a heavy revolver grasped tightly in his right hand.

"Son-of-a-bitch," he said again with much conviction.

Wetzel walked gingerly to the window, his toes still protruding from his socks, and said over his shoulder, "You already said that, Jimmy."

"You reckon he's gone?" Hawkins rasped.

"Maybeso," was all Wetzel managed to say. He wiped his trembling, sweating hands on the front of his long johns and turned to Hawkins standing behind him.

"Thanks for ... running him off," Wetzel stammered.

A quirk began at the corners of Hawkins' mouth. "That damned bear put a scald on your butt, Jack. Your trap door is hanging open—helluva sight for sore eyes, I'd say."

Wetzel quickly reached down, pulled the trap door closed and retorted, "Well, I don't recall anybody askin' you to say one way or the other, Jim Hawkins."

Hawkins laughed, grinning broadly. "Wait'll *this* story gets around the Forest."

Wetzel's hazel eyes weren't smiling. "Maybe the story of *you* having a firearm on duty against Forest Service policy would make an even better story, uh?"

A sobering new expression appeared on the Wilderness Patrolman's face. "Maybe we can come to a gentlemen's agreement an' keep tonight's happenings between the two of us?"

It was Wetzel's turn to smile. "Maybeso, Jim. Thanks for giving me a leg up tonight. And you were right about the kindling box." He walked into the kitchen holding the trap door in his left hand, opened the cabin door and stepped out into the night. The air felt cold to his clammy skin. The horses, mules and burros had begun to settle down in the corrals. He breathed in deep then released all the air in his lungs. *Hell of a time not to bring my dog along.*

Hawkins stood framed in the doorway, holding the revolver at his side. "Son ... of ... a bitch!" he murmured.

CHAPTER THIRTEEN

Roger O'Brian pulled his battered sombrero low over his tanned, weathered face as an early autumn wind began to pick up. *Damn these old, brittle bones o' mine*. He touched the spurs to his dun gelding as they climbed to the top of Goose Lake Ridge. The horse struggled through the rocks and steep grade. O'Brian wore his brown canvas ranch jacket and as he topped out on the ridge, he was glad that he had worn it. The air was cold. *Fall's comin', I reckon*.

From atop the long, flat ridge, he looked out over the country as his horse recovered from the steep climb. The Gila River cut a wide swath below him directly to the north, its steep rocky banks appearing much closer than they were in reality. He could clearly see where the river made a sharp bend at the confluence with Sapillo Creek to the east then he scanned westward to the dark crevasse of Turkey Creek and its confluence with the Gila River. Granny Mountain to the northeast beckoned to him as he sat horseback reflecting on the day.

He knew Brushy Mountain was located just north and on the other side of Granny. The old man recalled the story of James "Bear" Moore, a mountain man who emerged at the head waters of the Gila River in the latter part of the nineteenth century. Moore, unlike his counterparts Ben Lily and "Nat" Straw, did not care for notoriety, and in fact, much preferred to stay in the wilderness and away from other people. He had been attacked and severely wounded by a she bear. His face was left mangled and twisted to one side for the rest of his life and hence the name "Bear" by the locals. Ol' "Bear" Moore had lived in the wilderness until the time of his death in 1924. His body was found frozen in the snow about six miles from Alum Camp on the west side of Brushy Mountain overlooking Little Creek; they had buried him there. *Not so far from here as the crow flies,* O'Brian thought.

The old man had worked cattle in the Gila country most of his adolescent and all of his adult life. He had wanted nothing more. He felt he could relate to the old mountain men of yesteryear who had come to love this wilderness. He'd had a wonderful life with his wife of forty years until she'd become sick and died of the cancer. His whole world had turned upside down. In addition, the drought and the damn Forest Service were not making life easy for him. Jeez, it's gittin' hard to just make a livin' nowadays.

He had missed around ten head of his cows for some time and searched relentlessly for them to no avail. Seeing several cow tracks and fresh manure along the ridge top, he smiled, his weathered face wrinkling in the bright sunlight. Following the tracks for a ways on the ridge, he saw where the tracks traversed down off the ridge along Pack Saddle Canyon and toward the river. *More'n likely drinkin' at the river.* Dismounting, he stretched his chap-covered legs then checked and tightened the cinch on his horse.

As he rode down to the river taking his time, he thought about his daughter, Maggie, and wished with all his heart she would come out to the ranch and live with him. But she had refused him thus far by citing the remoteness and lack of a school close by as the reasons for her declining the invitation. She married Juan Garcia right out of high school against her father's wishes, and they'd had a son, Robbie, soon after. He was a good lookin' kid, too. O'Brian laughed out loud as he thought his grandson took after his ol' Grandpa.

He was not happy with Maggie working as a waitress in Dottie's Café or her living with that *viejita*, Doña Consuelo Vasquez. The old lady was pleasant enough, but there was something about her—a coldness behind those dark eyes. He couldn't put his finger on what bothered him about her, and it kept nagging at him from time to time. One thing was for sure—he didn't like all that *cuandera* healing crap that she was known for doing around town. Witchcraft is what it was as far as he was concerned. Supposedly, she practiced the ancient art of *cuaranderismo*, treating folks with physical, emotional, and dysfunctions of their soul or curses. He admitted to himself he didn't know all that much, only that the Mexican folk-healing had originated for treatment as far back as the Aztec days before the Spanish conquistadores arrived. Ah, to hell with the ol' witch anyhow.

He got to thinking of maybe selling his ranch and cattle and buying a little place in Silver City to finish out his aging years. Then maybe Maggie and the boy would come and live with him. Damned lonely life he led ... that was for damned sure. He knew Maggie prayed everyday for the Garcia boy to return home safe from Vietnam, but O'Brian figgered he was dead. Hell, it'd been two years since he was listed MIA. He admired his daughter for her belief in her husband and her turning to God for guidance. Hell, he hadn't set foot in a church after his wife had been taken from him and him being Irish and a staunch Catholic all his life. Maybe he'd have more time to attend church one of these days.

O'Brian's gray eyes searched the river bank for sign of his cattle as he noticed the water level was relatively low, the muddy brown water coursing along lazily to the west and eventually into Arizona where it merged with the San

Francisco River. Then on to the San Carlos Reservoir and by the time it reached the Phoenix area it became a dry wash nine times out of ten. He decided to ride eastward along the river bed toward Sapillo Creek. The cottonwood leaves had transitioned from green to yellow gold as had the sycamores with the occasional hackberries a bright red. In the midst of all the color contrasts along the river, he spotted something ahead that seemed out of place with its surroundings. *What the hell?*

He put his horse into an easy lope and covered the quarter mile quickly. His mouth dropped open as he rode up to the carcass hanging from a large limb of a sycamore tree. *Someone had butchered one of his cows!* Whoever it was had used a block and tackle to hoist the carcass high up in the air to butcher it. Rustling had not been a problem in these parts for many years, but O'Brian knew it still continued with a few cows being loaded into a trailer in the middle of the night occasionally. But this—

Riding slowly around the carcass, he observed the imprints of at least one man's boot; the soles appeared to be some type of hiking boot. The man, who ever he was, had traveled up and down the river numerous times from the carcass location. O'Brian reined his dun east, following the tracks at a trot.

He had traveled about a mile when he smelled wood smoke in the air. Pulling the horse up, he turned in the saddle to look behind him, his brow furrowed as he inherently felt something was wrong. Had he missed a side camp trail or someone hidden in the vegetation?

O'Brian thought he heard a soft shushing sound to his left, and as he started to turn back, something impacted his rib cage on the left side. A sharp, burning pain began in his chest and continued to the other side. His face took on a quizzical expression. Knowing something was terribly wrong he just couldn't determine what it was. Then he looked down at his right side. The jacket had been shoved sideways. Blood was spurting out of the hole in his shirt at his rib cage. He followed the life blood exiting his body toward the sycamore tree immediately to his right. A bloodied arrow was deeply embedded in the tree. Confusion showed plainly on his face as more blood continued to flow from his body and pain wracked his upper torso. A wave of nausea overcame him as he recognized both his lungs and possibly his heart had been nicked by the arrow.

It was all he could do to muster enough strength to look to his left. His eyes widened in horror as he saw the camouflaged figure, another arrow being fitted into the bow. *Jesus, Mary, mother of God!*

O'Brian slipped from his horse, dead before he hit the ground.

CHAPTER FOURTEEN
Fall, 1972

Robert McMurtry scratched his belly as he strode past the barn to begin feeding the twenty hound dogs chained at various locations adjacent to the barn at the Heart Bar Ranch. The hounds were a mix of black and tans, walkers, and red bones; all used by the Game Warden in tracking mountain lion in the Gila Wilderness. Weekend or not, he had to feed the dogs, horses and mules that belonged to the New Mexico Department of Game and Fish. He didn't kill the mountain lions he caught, only tranquilized and tagged them for future study.

He was beginning to thoroughly enjoy his new duty assignment in this dadjimmed New Mexico country. The Heart Bar Ranch headquarters sat just off Highway 15 near the bridge where the West and Middle Forks of the Gila River coursed under the two-lane highway that dead-ended a short distance later at Gila Center. Gila Center was home to a Visitor Center, government residences, a large helispot and fire crew quarters. McMurtry also enjoyed being a part of the small community of folks living in the isolated area. "Doc" Campbell's General Store was located several miles down the river and claimed to be the meetin' place for government and other local folks living in the Gila Center area. Campbell had arrived in the Gila country many years prior and established himself as an outfitter and guide, National Park Service caretaker of the Gila Cliff Dwellings, and then as proprietor of the general store. His two sons and two daughters assisted him in running the store and a lucrative outfitting business.

The Heart Bar Ranch had been a working cattle ranch in the old days replete with a U.S. Forest Service grazing permit for 1,500 cows within the established wilderness boundary. The New Mexico Game and Fish Department had attempted to re-establish elk in the forest for many years with the Forest Service objecting due to existing large cattle permits and the fact that cattle and elk competed for the same forage. In the 1940s, the Game and Fish Department decided to up and buy the Heart Bar Ranch—lock, stock, and barrel—including the Forest Service permit for 1,500 cattle grazing in the Gila Wilderness thereby eventually giving them the opportunity to re-introduce elk in the headwaters of the Gila in 1954.

A blue 1970 Pontiac four-door sedan turned off the highway and into the driveway. McMurtry quickly finished feeding the animals and sauntered over toward the old ranch house. His bearded face broke into a grin as he saw Juanita exit the driver's door, wave at him and open the rear passenger door allowing two young boys to jump out and run at him.

"Mac!" the boys yelled in unison.

"Wel-l-l now, boys," he said as he rumpled their close-cropped dark hair with his big coarse hand. "How the hell are ya anyhow?" Then McMurty saw another woman get out of the Pontiac from the front passenger side.

The oldest boy hugged the Game Warden, looked affectionately up at him and said solemnly, "Mother doesn't let us swear, Mac." The other boy grabbed his leg, pulling hard on it.

McMurtry knelt on one knee, eying the boy who had just spoken. "Wasn't planning on lettin' her in on the conversation, Jose. This here swearin's a man's business." His blue eyes twinkled as he peered into the boy's dark brown eyes. "Ya'll know what I mean—just between you, ol' Elfigo here, an' me—our little secret." He winked at Elfigo after placing an arm around Jose.

"I'm sure proud you boys could come an' see me." McMurtry stood peering again closely in the direction of the newly arrived car. "Who's the woman your mom brought with her this time, fellers?"

Elfigo spoke this time, after placing his little hands on his hips, "That's mom's cousin, Mac."

Jose was not to be outdone in the passing of state secrets to his friend. "Yeah, her name's Norma."

McMurtry patted the boys on their heads. His coarse face smiled as he adjusted his yellow ball cap, cocking it slightly to the right side. "You boys gonna hep me distract her just like we did with the last one your momma brought with her?"

Jose's face was pensive, his brown eyes serious in the morning light as he pursed his lips. "Mac, me an' Elfigo's been thinking. You got to offer us more'n a soda pop at Doc Campbell's store like last time."

Elfigo stood beside his brother, placed his arm over his brother's shoulder. He nodded his head with furrowed brow.

McMurtry rubbed his bearded chin, turned and spat behind him. Clearing his throat loudly, he said, "I reckon you boys got me in a pickle barrel beings that I sure 'nough need your hep." Rubbing the back of his neck with his left hand, he said, "Tell ya what, boys ... you hep me out with this here matter involving your momma, an' I'll take you both down to Campbell's store in my Game & Fish truck and buy each of ya a soda *and* a candy bar."

Jose nodded his head, licking his lips, but Elfigo the youngest demurred. It was his turn to rub his chin thoughtfully then the back of his neck. "I dunno, Mac. Mom was pretty mad at us last time—"

McMurtry knelt in front of both boys and pleaded, "Now come on fellers! Hep your ol' *compadre* just a little now." He placed a soft hand on each of the boy's shoulders. "Tell ya what, boys." He hesitated, again stroking his scruffy beard. "I'll run the si-reen on my truck as we drive over to the store! Is it a deal?"

Both boys grinned from ear to ear as they nodded the affirmative. All of the conspirators shook hands as a soft voice floated over to them from the car, "Roberto, are you coming?"

"Yes, ma'am, Juanita. Me an' the boys are headed your way." A huge grin appeared on his square, rough face and the blue eyes were smiling.

***

Juanita Flores stood inside the large screened back porch of the Heart Bar Ranch main house, her *prima* or cousin Norma beside her. The tin-roofed old ranch house was truly an *hacienda* to her; its odd "U" shape with two small front porches, each leading to a bedroom on either side of a grand living room replete with a large rock fireplace. Each bedroom had a fireplace of its own to warm its occupants in the cold of winter. A bunkhouse stood near the main house on the river side with the small, old original log bunkhouse to the east, which was no longer in use.

They had finished a bountiful supper of *enchiladas*, *frijoles*, rice and salad with a fried egg on top. She could hear her sons playing behind the bunkhouse near the river. The setting sun provided an orange glow to the west as she enjoyed the quiet, the peacefulness of the moment. *Thank you, God, for a wonderful day*.

Elfigo laughed aloud and his mother saw him standing near the bunkhouse. He waved at them and yelled, “Come on Norma! Come to the river with me and Jose. *Andelé*!”

Norma waved back and stepped from the porch. The boy ran up to her, grabbed her hand and pulled her with him out of sight behind the bunkhouse and on down to the river where his brother Jose was squealing and splashing in the river.

Juanita smiled as she started toward the screen door that had banged shut just moments before. A voice stopped her in her tracks. “Juanita?”

She turned and saw him step out onto the porch. The Game Warden tucked his big coarse hands into his overalls. *“Sí, Roberto.”*

His bright blue eyes peered at her then looked down at the porch. He started to reply, mumbled something, then said, “Meal sure was fine, Juanita. A man can really enjoy your home cookin’.”

Laughingly, she said, *“Why, gracias, Roberto.”*

“Thing is ... I’d ... uh, I’d like to ... talk to ya.” He bit his lower lip and shuffled his hunting boots. “That is if ya don’t mind bein’ alone with me for awhile.”

Her brow furrowed. “*Roberto*, I told you before. It eesn’t proper.”

“An’ I told you, Juanita.” Blue eyes met brown directly and held the gaze. “I would never harm you or your reputation. I just want to *talk* without one o’ your relatives listening in on every dadjimmed thang I say.”

She sighed deeply, placed her small brown hands in the back pockets of her faded Levi jeans. *“Bueño, Roberto.* Let’s talk, *mi amigo*. What ees on your mind?”

His gaze dropped. He couldn’t find the words. Hesitantly, he licked dry lips.

She said impatiently, *"Well?"*

He rubbed the back of his neck with his left hand, stuck his hands in and out of the pockets of his overalls several times. "The thang is ... well, I've come to ... to like you ... a whole bunch, Juanita," he blurted out.

Her brown eyes were smiling before her pretty mouth followed suit. "I like you, too, *Roberto*."

McMurtry's bearded, coarse face broke into a grin, eyes wide. "An' I like them dadjimmed boys o' yours, too. A whole bunch."

She said nothing, allowing him time to fidget with his cap, first tipping the old yellow cap with the "Tennessee Vols" insignia back then cocking it slightly to the right.

"Thing is ... I'd like to ... marry you, Juanita."

Still she said nothing as her heart pounded in her breast.

The Game Warden turned away, his head down. "I ain't much to look at ... I know that more'n anybody. An' I ain't got much in the way o' material things."

She started to speak, but he held up his hand stopping her. "Lemme git it all out, Juanita. Now that I'm all warmed up and blabbing like a dadjimmed fool."

Walking to the other end of the porch, he stood there looking out over the country near the river as a red-tailed hawk circled above then he turned. "I'd be a good husband to ya, an' a good daddy to them boys."

Juanita walked over to him, stood on her tiptoes and kissed him on the cheek. Placing her hands on her hips, her solemn dark brown eyes held his blue. "After my divorce—*que horror!* I thought I would *never* marry *otra vez, pero* ... you are a good man *y creo que te amo."*

Puzzled, he blurted out, "I don't reckon I understand all that Mexican talk, Juanita."

She threw back her head and laughed out loud. "Well ... ees about *dadjimmed* time you learned, *Roberto!*"

He took off his cap, grasping it tightly in both hands. "Y'all marry an ol' country boy like me?" His hunting boots shuffled on the cement floor of the porch.

She looked at him longingly, understanding fully the true goodness in this coarse rough man, knowing without question that he would always take care of her and her boys. "Gracias, for thinking of me and the boys, *Roberto*. I theenk veery much of you, but I need time."

His blue eyes softened. "Well-l-l, you've not said no."

Juanita smiled. "No, *Roberto*. I haf not said, no."

"Wel-l-l, I'll be dadjimmed." It was his turn to smile then he kissed her gently on her lips.

CHAPTER FIFTEEN

A cool fall breeze blew in the open driver's window of Wetzel's old truck, rustling the collar of his flannel shirt as he descended the high country of Pinos Altos to Silver City. He thought Pinos Altos probably looked pretty much like it did nearly 150 years ago when gold was first found in the area by Spanish and Mexican miners. The Anglos had rediscovered the gold in 1859 and for a while it was called Birchville after the first man to find gold there. The fierce-some Apache warriors chased most of the miners clear of the area for several years, but it was re-established in 1866 as Pinos Altos and this time the Spanish name stuck as its official handle.

Simon and Garfunkel were singing, "*Mrs. Robinson*", on the radio. He turned the channel knob to the Arenas Valley country western station. Tammy Wynette crooned "*D-I-V-O-R-C-E*" over the airway. The headlights cut through the inky darkness as the heavy growth of Ponderosa pine trees gave way to much smaller piñon pine and alligator juniper then to the cleared residential areas lining Highway 15. The sky, clear and bright with stars and a full moon, made the evening drive enjoyable.

He geared down at the first stoplight then turned right onto Highway 180 or Silver Heights Boulevard and drove south toward downtown Silver City. Several children were playing along the street. A pretty little Hispanic girl with black hair and rosy cheeks looked at him and smiled as he drove by. He returned the smile and waved to her. A slender black man sporting a black fedora on his head and wearing a long black overcoat with a white scarf around his neck strode hurriedly past the little girl, seemingly going nowhere and everywhere at the same time. *Johnny Banks!*

Wetzel shouted, "Howdy, Johnny!" out the truck window. The man smiled and waved as he continued on down the street. A man who many said just wasn't all there mentally. Wetzel grinned. *Maybe we're the ones who aren't all there, come to think of it.* Banks lived with his mother and grandmother, and as far as Wetzel knew, he didn't bother anyone in town. Just made his daily rounds all over town and daily to the University where everyone welcomed him as the perpetual student for the past 20 years.

Silver City, New Mexico, had sprung up overnight during the summer of 1870 with the discovery of silver and the ensuing onslaught of miners trying to get rich quickly. They were, of course, followed by the merchants, who had decided early on to build a town that would last. They created the townsite by laying out the streets running north, south, east, and west just like the cities back east. In 1895 and again in 1903, flash floods gouged out a huge ditch in what was then Main Street. Wetzel noted only one original brick building along Main Street still remained. The rest of Main Street had simply been turned backwards, with business continuing through the back door.

Turning onto Bullard Street, Wetzel progressed through the quiet downtown area illuminated by street lights. A cute blonde lady wearing a short skirt walked along the sidewalk holding a poodle in tow. The young woman waved at him seductively. Wetzel couldn't help but look at the pretty woman then the dog. The poodle was dressed up in a little hat with ribbons hanging down, a strap under its chin with a big rose attached on top. Most everyone in town knew it was Madam Millie's way of announcing that a new girl was now in residence, ready for business. Wetzel grinned broadly at the woman then waved at the little dressed up dog. *What had some of the guys on the fire crew said the dog's name was? Lulu?*

As he exited Bullard onto Market Street, he could see the bright neon lights of the Buffalo Bar just down the street; the parked cars and motorcycles signifying an active, busy night. The bar's name came from an old buffalo head located inside the establishment behind the bar with red light bulbs for eyes that could be switched on and off at the proprietor's discretion.

Proceeding west on Market Street and passing Saint Vincent de Paul Catholic Church, Wetzel hesitated at the stop sign, looking both ways, then crossed the street and parked behind a dark green Dodge sedan on the north side. The small single-story, flat-roofed apartment duplex stood out in the moonlight. Each apartment was designated by door and accompanying porch light. Wetzel tipped his hat back on his head, straightened his new shirt, and polished his Roper boots against his Wrangler jeans then he walked up to the apartment on the right and knocked.

Moments passed. No one came to the door; he reached to knock on the screen door again. The porch light came on, the interior door opened slightly, and Wetzel could see the security chain was still attached inside. A female voice crackled in the stillness of the night, *"¿Que quieres?"*

"I'm looking for Maggie O'Brian, ma'am," said Wetzel.

Silence. A man laughed loudly from the adjacent apartment and a woman giggled annoyingly.

"¿Quien es?" The hard voice carried authority.

"I'm Jack Wetzel, ma'am." He shuffled his boots on the doorstep. *"¿Doña Consuelo Vasquez?"*

The security chain was removed, the interior door opened to display a tall dark slender woman. She did not reach to unlatch the screen door. The dark deep-set eyes were hard and unsmiling, the mouth's thin lips set cruelly in a shallow face that was wrinkled by a lifetime of incessant wind and sun. Shoulder length gray and white hair was pulled back from her gaunt face. Adjusting a dark, blue sweater to better cover herself, she said sharply, "*Sí.* I am *Doña Consuelo.*"

Wetzel removed his Stetson and smiled. Hazel eyes regarded the simmering dark brown eyes of the older lady. They stood there, surveying one another, and Wetzel felt as though her piercing eyes were peering deep into his soul. "I'm an old friend of Maggie's, ma'am. I'd sure like to see her tonight if it's not too much trouble."

A quirk pulled at the corner of the older lady's mouth. The eyes softened but remained unsmiling as they surveyed him from head to toe: the disheveled brown hair, honest face, the tall frame dressed in jeans and boots. "Maggie's not here, Jack Wetzel." She pointed toward the church. "You'll find her praying ... over there." The door slammed shut, and he heard first the dead bolt then the chain lock being replaced.

He just stood there, hat in hand, not sure of exactly what to do. Then he remembered his mother's recent words, "You go see Maggie, son. If she needs help ... why, you give it to her, and the boy, too."

Wetzel turned and walked slowly back to the street past his parked truck, crossed the street to the church. He stood silently in front of Saint Vincent de Paul Catholic Church. The church stood out like a medieval castle in the darkened night. The high domes atop the structure topped with crosses stood as tall sentinels guarding the sacred premises.

He was plagued with a feeling of uncertainty, and doubt crept into his head as if he was doing something wrong. He turned to go, thought better of it, and began to climb the numerous narrow concrete steps. A soft voice murmured to him as he labored up endless steps to reach the very top. *It's all right, Jack.*

He found the main door open and slightly ajar. After taking off his hat, he stood there in the quiet of the night. The evening breeze toyed at his thick hair and brushed against his cheek. There was no sound inside the church. He took a deep breath of fresh air, exhaled, and stepped into the church. Hearing his heart pound inside his chest, he moved forward toward the many rows of wooden pews. They, in turn, directed him from both sides toward the ornate, white altar which was located at the front of the church. The Stations of the Cross were aligned on both walls reminding Wetzel of Christ's brutal march to his fatal crucifixion that saved all mankind. He saw Maggie kneeling at the altar, her scarf-covered head bowed in prayer in front of the massive statue of Sacred Heart of Jesus.

Pausing momentarily halfway to the altar, Wetzel felt as if he were imposing on something very private; he lost his courage and turned to leave. Then something caught his eye. The lit candles on either side of the altar wavered and flickered then both flickered noticeably again, seemingly beckoning him forward. His brow furrowed, he bit nervously at his lower lip. The candles flickered yet again. He hadn't imagined it; somehow it was real. Or was it?

He gained enough courage to step forward again to within a few feet of the kneeling woman. He licked his dry lips, grasped his hat tightly with both hands as he heard her sob silently. Wanting to console his friend, he said softly, "Maggie, it's Jack Wetzel."

She turned quickly, eyes wide and mouth open. As she saw the young man standing there, she covered her mouth and stifled the sound about to be emitted. Her red shoulder length hair was pulled back from her face into a pony tail and covered by a bright blue scarf. The slender figure that Wetzel recalled from high school days was filled out, displaying a pleasant transition into womanhood. Maggie wore faded Levis and a white blouse covered by a denim jumper.

Her face brightened and smiled at him. The pretty green eyes were smiling too, as she wiped at her tear-streaked face. "Jack! Is it *you*?"

Wetzel grinned as he peered at his friend. "I reckon so, Maggie girl." There was character in the set of her mouth and chin and grace in the outlines of her body.

She ran at him, almost knocking him off balance, and hugged him tightly. He held her close, feeling her warmth. "Oh ... Jack—" And she started crying again. Looking up, Wetzel saw the lit candles at the altar were no longer wavering. He felt her body against his, smelled her hair as he pulled her even tighter to him. Then he was ashamed of his thoughts toward another man's wife—his best friend's wife—and he stood back away from her, hands awkwardly at his sides.

They sat outside the church on the very top step. The stars twinkled in the sky; the lights of downtown illuminated the skyline. Answering Maggie's many questions Wetzel told her that after his stint in the Army, he had attended New Mexico State University on the GI bill. He'd finished in four years with a degree in Range Management. After graduation, he had applied with the U.S. Forest Service and received an offer for a job, not as a Range Conservationist as he'd wanted, but a job nonetheless. And, yes, he liked his job at Gila Center. His mother was doing just fine. And, yes, he'd been glad to help her dad out with the fence work for the Forest Service allotment.

"And you, Maggie? What have you been up to since high school?"

"Juan and I married right after you left for Viet Nam." She pursed her lips then spoke, "He got a job out at Tyrone—a good job at the mine. I was pregnant and life was going so well for us, Jack." The brightened eyes dulled, showing her sadness. He felt a lump in his throat as he saw her struggle to speak, but he said nothing.

She sighed looking out into the night. "Then he ... he was drafted and left for Nam." She bit her lip, the green eyes closed. "He ... never came back ... didn't even get to see our son." Dropping her head to her knees, she cried out loudly in the night.

Wetzel swallowed hard and softly rubbed her back. The crying stopped. Silence. Still he knew to say nothing.

"If only they'd told me he was dead, Jack. I know it sounds terrible, but at least there would be some sort of ... closure or something. You know, time to move on in life as hard as that would be. But he's been missing in action for two years. I don't even know if he's dead or alive!"

"I'm so sorry, Maggie," murmured Wetzel.

Green eyes met hazel. "You're a good friend, Jack. You were always there for me and Juan." She reached out and held his hands in hers. "I pray everyday that Juan will return to me and Robbie. I just have to believe that he's still alive."

Wetzel put his arms around Maggie's shoulders. Softly, he said, "Maggie, I haven't been to church since I don't know when, but if you help me ... why, I'll pray with you for Juan's return—to us."

The breeze gently picked up out of the south at their feet beckoning them back into the small church that sat atop one of the many wind-swept hillsides in Silver City; a beautiful church built centuries ago to serve those in need just as it now served a modern population with strikingly similar needs.

Wetzel stood. “Come on, kid. Let’s say our prayers then I’ll walk you home, uh?”

CHAPTER SIXTEEN

Wetzel drew deeply on the Lucky Strike cigarette then tucked it into the corner of his mouth, the smoke drifting from his nose. He enjoyed the coolness of the early fall morning. Vehicles passed along Highway 180 behind his parked Forest Service truck. He figured they were headed either into Silver City or the other direction toward Arenas Valley, Bayard, and maybe even south to Deming.

Dottie's Café was located along the south side of Highway 180 and just north of the turn-off to Hudson Street. It was an excellent place to have a hearty breakfast and served equally well as an ideal meeting place. Wetzel didn't frequent the café often, but it had been selected by Deputy Sheriff Don Ramirez for the two of them and New Mexico State Policeman Steve Hunt to discuss business.

He pulled his Stetson lower on his face, the shadow lengthening on his tanned face beneath the hat. Dressed in his Forest Service uniform and green jacket with the shoulder insignia, he placed his foot, protected by a dusty Packer boot, on the back bumper of the truck. He watched the uniform-clad deputy step out of his patrol car in the parking lot some twenty feet distant. Don Ramirez had played football with Wetzel in high school and they knew each other fairly well. A tackle on the team's offensive line, Ramirez was as stoutly built as Wetzel was slender. His arms bulged under his uniform shirt and his thick, sturdy legs carried the heavy-set torso well. As the young deputy approached, Wetzel extended his hand saying, "Howdy,

Don. *¿Como estas?*"

Ramirez grinned as he shook hands. "*Bien*, Wetzel. How you been, partner?"

Wetzel liked the firm handshake and the smiling brown eyes that met his hazel eyes directly.

"Good." Wetzel's cigarette bobbed along his lips from one corner of his mouth to the other. "What's this meetin' all about, Don?"

"Our department needs your help, Jack."

"Oh—?"

A black State Police car pulled into the parking lot, and a short, stocky officer stepped out. He placed his black dress cap on his head over close-cropped sandy hair. Looking very official in his black uniform replete with badge, black leather shoulder strap, belt and holster, black creased trousers with a stripe down each side, and polished black dress boots, Officer Steve Hunt made quite an impressive sight that fall September day.

The three men filed into the restaurant, the bell on the entry door jingling cheerfully as they made their way to an open booth in the corner, Wetzel trailing in the rear.

A leering voice called out loudly, "Hey ... *war hero!* Been saving anybody lately?" The bitterness and hatred exuded from each word spoken.

Wetzel saw Joe Peach seated at a booth on the far side of the café. He was dressed in a uniform as well, but it was unkempt, the middle shirt button popped loose from the pressure of a huge belly that protruded over his Sam Brown duty belt. One of a handful of officers working for the City Police Department in Silver City, New Mexico, Peach was seated with three young men. Wetzel recognized them as trouble-makers for the most part. Two had long hair down to their shoulders. A bearded man wore camouflaged pants, the others bell-bottom jeans. Wetzel had heard through the grapevine that Peach bullied the prostitutes at Millies and had even attempted extortion on the madam herself.

Wetzel didn't respond but continued toward the booth where Ramirez and Hunt were seating themselves.

"HEY! I'm talking to you." Peach's voice carried across the room.

Wetzel turned as he said softly, "I can hear you, Joe. I'm just surprised you can talk so well with those dentures you wear these days."

Peach looked at the two officers with Wetzel then glared at him, eyes blazing with hatred, but he said nothing as Wetzel continued over to the booth where the other officers waited. Ramirez frowned. "What was *that* all about?"

"Nothing ... just a little past history is all," said Wetzel as he sat and picked up a menu.

"Oh, yeah. I remember now. You knocked out all his teeth in high school."

The State Police Officer couldn't resist the question, "You *what?*"

Wetzel didn't answer.

Ramirez said, "I'll tell you the story one day when you have lots of time, Steve."

Hunt peered intently at Wetzel. "*Are* you a war hero?"

Wetzel exhaled turning a coffee cup right side up. "Nope."

Ramirez interjected, "Why would you say that, Jack?"

Wetzel thought of Weapons Platoon Sergeant Merrell. He sighed. "Because I was there. I fought with real heroes, and I'm here to tell you I'm not one of 'em."

A startled loud gasp was uttered then the sound of dishes breaking loudly as they came in contact with the hard, concrete floor. Wetzel saw the busboy had fallen, the ceramic dishes he had been carrying shattered into many pieces and scattered in various directions. A boy, who Wetzel had seen in the restaurant on several previous occasions and had appeared mentally challenged, now lay sprawled on the floor his eyes wide with fright. He could clearly see the boy didn't know what to do. Confusion, fear, embarrassment, and anger totally incapacitated him for the moment.

Laughter came from the booth next to the boy where Peach and his friends sat. The man in camouflaged pants laughed the loudest and said contemptuously, "You *stupid* idiot! You better watch where you're going, boy."

Wetzel eased from his seat, and walked to the boy. As he knelt on one knee beside him, Wetzel placed his hand on the shaking shoulders and saw tears trickling down the scared pale face.

Arrogantly, Peach said to Wetzel, "What the hell d'you think you're doing?"

Ignoring the question, he said to the boy, "I'm Wetzel. What's your name?"

"Will ... ie," the boy sobbed.

"Well, Willie. What say, let's you and me clean up this mess, uh?" Wetzel knelt down on both knees and began picking up pieces of plates.

A belligerent voice bellowed out, "What the *hell's* going on here? Willie, you—" The proprietor had arrived from the kitchen.

Wetzel spoke sharply, "No harm done." The hazel eyes were hard, icy.

Camouflaged pants snorted. "The stupid, clumsy oaf can't keep his feet."

Willie turned toward his boss and shouted while pointing, "*He* tripped me!"

"Why you lying little—"

"I need some help over here, Willie," interposed Wetzel.

The boy looked at Wetzel busily picking up the larger ceramic pieces and placing them on an adjacent table. He wiped his tears away, grinned and began emulating his benefactor. "You betcha, Wetzel."

As Wetzel continued working, he spoke to the proprietor, "Me and Willie ... we sure could use a broom, dust pan, and a trash can."

The man grunted, said nothing, turned abruptly and disappeared into the back of the restaurant.

Hearing soft footsteps, Wetzel looked up into pretty green eyes set in a freckled face that was surrounded by a full head of shoulder-length red hair. Maggie O'Brian's furrowed brow and narrowed eyes studied him carefully with new found respect.

"Hi, Jack."

"Maggie! How are you?" He said as he stood holding pieces of ceramic in his hands. He set them on the table, took the coffee pot from her, and handed it to a startled Deputy Ramirez who was now standing beside him. Then he hugged her tightly. Holding her close, she felt so good to him. Deputy Ramirez stood holding the coffee pot a surprised expression on his face. He said nothing.

Peach's cronies stood and began to depart the booth. Snide comments and laughter drifted over their shoulders. Camouflaged pants kicked several pieces of ceramic as he exited with the others to the front of the restaurant. Peach stood briefly next to Maggie and nodded his thick head toward Wetzel. "What's *he* got that I haven't?"

Seemingly puzzled, she stood without responding then said softly, "Me, Joe." She swallowed hard as she peered into Wetzel's eyes. "He's got me."

Deputy Ramirez grinned. Officer Peach snorted as he turned to leave. "Screw the both of you!"

The proprietor returned and they all pitched in to clean the mess on the floor. Maggie returned with them to the table, and she told Wetzel she had been working at the café for several months. Ramirez asked after Robbie. Maggie responded her son was doing well. Four years old going on five.

"Any news on Juan?" Wetzel asked and regretted it immediately.

The smile faded from her radiant face and eyes. "No, nothing."

A loud voice shouted from the kitchen, "Hey, Maggie. Get to work! If you wanna stand around and talk, do it somewhere else on your own dime."

She retrieved the coffee pot and began filling their cups. All the orders placed, she turned to Wetzel. "Will you have some time to talk tonight?"

"Not tonight, Maggie. We've got plans for him," interjected Deputy Ramirez. "That is if he'll help us find where your father is hiding out. We need a good tracker."

A concerned look on her face, she said, "The lady who cleans his house weekly reported he wasn't there when she arrived to clean, and it looked as though he'd been gone for at least a day." Her pretty brow furrowed as she looked over her shoulder at the kitchen expecting to get yelled at again. "He might've been thrown or something, Jack."

"He'll turn up, Maggie. I'm sure he's okay." Wetzel looked at the two officers and grinned. "He's a tough ol' bird, and he knows the country better'n all of us put together."

Maggie asked they keep her informed, and returned to the kitchen. State Police Officer Hunt leaned forward on his elbows across the table from Wetzel. "I was thinking of getting a couple of posse search teams together and a helicopter."

Wetzel thought a minute. "Why don't you hold off on calling 'em out just yet. Go ahead and put 'em on standby if you want, but I don't want people out at the ranch wallering around any sign Mr. O'Brian may have left. I'll head out to the ranch tonight and be ready to check for sign and begin tracking at first light tomorrow."

Officer Hunt rubbed his square jaw. "And the helicopter?"

"You goin' to use one from the Forest Service helitack base?"

"Yeah. Already got permission from the Supervisor's Office to use it in the wilderness."

Wetzel drank heartily of the hot coffee. It had never failed to taste good to him in the mornings. "That's great, Steve. It'll only be a few minutes flight time over Brushy Mountain to where I think we'll find him. Can you spare me one of your portable radios?"

"Done. What other resources do you need?"

Placing the coffee mug on the table, Wetzel peered at Deputy Ramirez. "I'd like Don to go with me if he's got the time."

Deputy Ramirez nodded his head in the affirmative as Officer Hunt's puzzled face asked, "That's *all* you'll need?"

"I reckon so. If I need additional help, I can call you on your handy-dandy walkie talkie."

Officer Hunt grinned broadly as he saw Maggie approaching with his plate full of huevos rancheros bathed in red chile alongside hot fried potatoes, and hot tortillas. "I think I'm going to like working with you, Wetzel."

Wetzel thought of where the old rancher might have

gone and fervently hoped no one had obliterated any fresh tracks. The weather should cooperate according the latest forecast. His thoughts were interrupted as Maggie brushed against him placing his bacon and scrambled eggs with green chile on the table. He smiled a quick assurance into the worried green eyes.

CHAPTER SEVENTEEN

Dawn couldn't come soon enough for Wetzel. He'd arrived at the O'Brian ranch the previous night with Deputy Sheriff Don Ramirez. They found the rancher's horse standing near the corral, reins broken and missing from the bridle. Then they saw blood on the saddle. It had been a sleepless, worrisome night for both lawmen, but they knew better than to try and track at night.

Wetzel placed a second water bottle in his backpack, secured the top flap then tied his rolled denim jacket on top. The fall air had a chill to it, and Wetzel shivered slightly without his jacket on. He knew it would be foolish to wear it while hiking uphill. Dark skies turning pink began to usher in the dawn as he peered at Ramirez, who swung his backpack up and onto his large shoulders. "We'd best be getting' to it, Don. Are you set to go?"

The deputy hooked his thumbs in the shoulder straps of his pack. His worried face showed deep concern for the welfare of the rancher. "Yep." Walking over to his patrol car, he reached inside and brought out a 1911 .45 caliber pistol and a Ruger Mini-14 rifle. Returning, he handed the pistol to Wetzel. "Best take it, Jack. We don't know what we're up against out there."

"I never had much use for a pistol in the war, Don. The officers were always trying to get me to carry one on point ... I never did." He sighed. "I've done enough killin' to last me a lifetime. I want no more of it."

"They're reliable enough," Ramirez said referring to

the pistol and ignoring his friend's latest comment as he remembered to close the door to the sedan. "Just don't forget to take the safety off if you have to shoot the damn thing." He placed his hand on the .357 revolver he carried in a leather holster at his side as he watched Wetzel hesitate then place the pistol inside his pack and swing it over his shoulders.

Wetzel whistled softly and tapped his left hand against his right shoulder. O'Brian's old stock dog appeared, tail wagging, and sat beside him. Wetzel bent down and rubbed the graying head. "Come on, Pepper, let's go find Mr. O'Brian."

Wetzel circled the ranch buildings looking for sign, and easily determined the only route the rancher had followed. They followed the obvious horse tracks leading up to Goose Lake Ridge to the north, laboring up the steep grade toward the ridge top. When they stopped to catch their breath from time to time, the old dog would race past them only to find a shady spot to rest a short distance from the trackers.

On one such break Ramirez removed his pack, took a drink from his water bottle and wiped his mouth with the back of his hand. "You ought to get a *real* job, Wetzel. Come to work for the Sheriff's Office with me. You'd move up fast in the organization." He pulled his straw hat down to better shade his face. "Me ... I plan to be Sheriff of Grant County someday."

Wetzel grinned at his friend. "Naw, I reckon not, Don. I kinda like working for the Forest Service. Thanks just the same."

The deputy shrugged. "Suit yourself. Nobody likes the damn Forest Service."

"Oh, there's a few that do," retorted a grinning Wetzel.

He stood stretching his tall, slender frame. “Not many, now that I think about it, but a few.”

“How the hell did you get that job anyhow,” asked the deputy.

“I sent in a job interest card to the Civil Service in Albuquerque and a few months later they hired me.”

“Seems easy enough.”

“It was. Not like the old timers in the early 1900s from what my dad told me,” said Wetzel.

“How’s that?”

“My father said the old Rangers had to take a written exam starting in 1906, and they didn’t have multiple choice questions back in the day. Questions requiring written answers like: How many men does it take to run 10,000 foot sawmill? How do you fight wildfires? Surveying and mining questions, too. Then the applicants had to saddle a horse and demonstrate how to ride and pack.”

Ramirez grunted as he lifted his pack to his shoulders. “You won’t have to do all that shit to become a deputy, Jack.”

Wetzel laughed without replying. He turned and trudged uphill his eyes glued to the sign ahead of him on the hillside.

The sun was high in the sky overhead when they topped out on Goose Lake Ridge and started down toward the Gila River descending Packsaddle Canyon on the north side of the ridge. So far Wetzel had observed two sets of horse tracks; one horse going and returning via the same route. What the hell happened to the ol’ man? Had he been thrown and hurt badly? If so, why the blood on his saddle? The more he thought about the possibilities, the more it made no sense to him at all. He knew the old man well, and it was difficult to believe he had met with an accident, as proficient as he was in the wilderness and horseback.

It was very steep and rocky descending to the Gila River and Wetzel had to pay close attention to any rolling rocks that Deputy Ramirez sent his way inadvertently. Ramirez would yell, "Rock!" and Wetzel would scramble out of the way, the rocks bouncing high in the air down into the steep canyon. It seemed as though it took longer in the descent from the ridge than the ascent might have, but finally they heard running water in the river bottom amongst the thick vegetation.

Wetzel sat on his heels surveying sign along the sand bar leading to the east along the Gila River toward the confluence with Sapillo Creek. Puzzled, he removed his Stetson and scratched his head. He looked up at Deputy Ramirez. "I don't get it, Don. There's no sign of the horse going up or down the river from here. In fact, there's no sign of any wildlife along this stretch of the river either."

He stood, replacing his hat squarely on his head. Motioning with his hand, he pointed in the direction of Turkey Creek. "Why don't you check for sign a ways down river? I'll head the other way, and maybe between the two of us, we'll find something."

Ramirez nodded. "Okay, Jack." He slung the rifle over his shoulder and turned to look at Wetzel. "You be careful. I can't read sign like you do, but I'd say someone brushed out all the tracks."

Wetzel's hazel eyes displayed no emotion. "Maybeso."

It didn't take long to find overturned river rocks and other sign left by the horse's shod hooves. Wetzel's grim face was determined as he strode along the riverbank following the disturbed sign. He progressed about a mile and stood observing an area where he would've ridden had he been horseback. It was obvious someone had used cut vegetation in an attempt to sweep out the horse's tracks. Whoever it was had gotten sloppy or tired in their covering of the numerous tracks as they had progressed up river.

Withdrawing a Lucky Strike cigarette from his shirt pocket, Wetzel watched several band-tailed pigeons fly past him as he lit it with a match from the same pocket. O'Brian's old dog Pepper trotted up and lay down beside Wetzel. Squatting on his heels, he drew deeply on the cigarette, listening intently his eyes seeing everything. There was a bad feeling deep in his gut and it emanated out increasing his anxiety. *What the hell's goin' on here, anyhow?* He hadn't felt raw fear in his stomach since Nam. *Why would someone want to hurt the ol' man? Hell, he was cantankerous as all get out, but harmless.* The cigarette bobbed back and forth between his lips from one side to the other as he sat quietly smoking and thinking about what the hell he had gotten himself into.

He observed several blood spots on an upturned river rock then the ground disturbance someone had attempted to remove but could not because of the actions of a panicked horse at that location. A shudder ran through Wetzel's body. Still he sat smoking, listening, not moving. The old dog moved closer, his head up, ears tipped forward facing north. A low growl began in his throat; it ceased as Wetzel placed a hand on his neck and hissed.

The faint smell of smoke and burning hide filled Wetzel's nostrils as a breeze picked up from the north then dissipated as the wind changed direction. Wetzel ground the cigarette out on the sole of his Packer boot, stood, adjusted his backpack on his shoulders, and walked approximately thirty yards to the north side of the riverbank. It was here that he clearly saw the remnants of a vibram shoe print beside a cottonwood tree. Only the toe portion of one print remained, the rest had been brushed out. He stood behind the partial print careful not to disturb it and looked back from whence he'd come.

He took his time canvassing the area south of his position, his brow furrowed. *What am I missing?* It was apparent to him that something tragic had occurred at that location, but what? Did the old man fall off his horse and hit his head? Was he pulled off? So intense was his thought, Wetzel only faintly heard Deputy Ramirez calling his name from downriver. He didn't respond. The skin prickled on the back of his neck as his horrified gaze centered on a large cottonwood tree across from him and the broken end of a bloody, impaled arrow shaft.

CHAPTER EIGHTEEN

Officer Joe Peach grinned as he pulled the collar of his blue Silver City Police uniform jacket up around his bulging neck. The stupid son-of-a-bitch had actually agreed to meet with him at his choice of locations. He maneuvered the police sedan south on Bullard Ave., crossed the railroad tracks then turned onto Mill Street under the recently built re-routed Highway 90 and drove easterly past the old train station that had been closed for several years. He continued down the graveled street where there were no street lights. Several huge metal storage buildings stood out eerily in the moonlit night.

Painstakingly, he ensured there were no other vehicles in the vicinity by driving up to Bard Street, returning to check if there were any parked vehicles with occupants near any of the metal storage buildings. Convinced there were none, he switched off his headlights then backed his patrol sedan behind the metal building closest to Mill Street out of sight.

He waited ten minutes in the shadows before he heard the sound of a motor vehicle traveling his direction. As the known vehicle approached his position, he stepped from behind the building and quickly directed it to where his sedan was parked. The unmarked police sedan came to rest adjacent to his marked rig. A tall, muscular man sporting a crew haircut and wearing a white long-sleeved dress shirt and cotton slacks stepped out of the car and strode to where Peach stood.

"How the hell are ya, Lieutenant?" asked Peach with a sneer on his face.

The man peered at the officer then spoke, "I'm fine, Joe." He looked all around where they were parked and hooked his thumbs in his pants pockets. "Why meet here, Joe?" he asked quizzedly.

"Why not?"

A frown formed on the good looking man's face replaced by a hardening of the eyes. "I don't have time for games, Peach. Get to the point."

Peach's large bulbous head leaned forward in the moonlight. "Oh, I will Lieutenant Harding. Rest assured I will get to the point."

Placing his right hand on the revolver at his side, he said, "My sources tell me you've been investigating me, Charlie. That so?"

"As Internal Affairs Officer, it's my responsibility to ensure that none of our officers are working outside the law."

"I didn't ask you for a job description," snarled Peach.

Hardings' voice was sharp, "You watch your mouth." His hands balled up into fists at his side.

Peach's voice was conciliatory. " Hell, I don't mean nothin', Lieutenant. Just tryin' to find out if mah job is in jeopardy. That's all." He placed both hands in his coat pockets.

Lieutenant Harding folded his arms against his chest. "Look Peach, I can't guarantee anything except that if you cooperate in the investigation, I'll make sure the prosecutor is aware of your help."

Peach said nothing. Sensing compliance, Harding continued, "Tell me who your contacts are, where the marijuana fields are located, Joe."

"I dunno, Lieutenant." Peach withdrew his left hand

from the jacket pocket and scratched his chin thoughtfully. "What I really need is for you to tell me who's been rattin' me out."

"Even if that were so, you know I couldn't tell you, Joe."

"Sure ya can, Charlie," returned Peach. "You give me the information I want, an' I share some of the profits with you." Peach grinned at his astonished superior. "What's the matter? Conscience botherin' ya?"

Lieutenant Harding's eyes were on fire. "You arrogant, rotten bastard!" He turned to leave.

"Oh, Lieutenant—"

Harding turned and found himself uncomfortably close to the larger patrolman. So close he could smell body odor emanating from the man. He attempted to step back and away as Peach moved in close, his right hand in his pocket. Lieutenant Harding felt the muzzle of a revolver against his stomach through the officer's coat pocket. The roar of the .38 revolver muffled his response. A hot burning sensation pierced his body followed by an agonizing pain in his abdomen then his back. Staggering backward, he stumbled and fell to the ground as his legs melted out from under him.

Officer Peach knelt close to the shocked, moaning officer and calmly searched him for weapons. Finding a .38 in an ankle holster, he retrieved it and placed it in his back pocket. Chuckling, he leaned in close to a gasping Lieutenant Harding. "Now ... *you* listen to me, you piece of shit," he whispered contemptuously. You'll tell me everything I need to know or die a slow, horrible death before I'm done with you."

Gritting his teeth, Harding hissed, "Go to hell!"

Peach laughed aloud. "Charlie, Charlie. You mucky mucks never cease to amaze me." Sighing, he pulled the previously discharged .38 from his jacket pocket and shoved it into Harding's groin. Cocking the hammer, he rasped, "Now start talkin' or I'll make you suffer *big* time before you die!"

Lieutenant Harding gazed into the hate-filled eyes of his subordinate. Summoning all his strength, he spat directly at those eyes as he braced himself for the unexpected. The gunshot reverberated out into the still moonlit night followed by subsequent screams of a man in agony.

CHAPTER NINETEEN

Wetzel and Deputy Sheriff Ramirez stood over the still-smoking fire pit. Although the fire had died down considerably, the stench of burning hide staunchly remained and the men stood on the windward side of the fire. Following sign they had hiked up a side canyon heading north from the river toward Granny Mountain. Approximately a half mile in, where the canyon forked, they found the camp. It appeared to Wetzel that one man had been living there for several months evidenced by one particular track found everywhere in and around the campsite—a vibram soled boot, size 10. There were other infrequent tracks of men as well at the site.

Finding a stick, Wetzel poked at the near dead fire and bones. A cloud of ashes rose in the air as the wind momentarily changed direction. He directed his comments at Ramirez, his eyes on the fire pit. "Better let Mac at the Heart Bar know of this poaching, Don." Burnt deer hooves lay to the outside of the fire perimeter, and many large bones remained unconsumed by the huge fire that had been built.

Ramirez moved out of the smoke as it changed direction in the swirling wind. "Why in the hell would a man burn up game that he's poached, Jack?" He slung the Mini-14 rifle on his shoulder. He didn't wait for an answer. "You reckon whoever was here hightailed it out?"

Wetzel said nothing as he continued poking and spreading the pile of bones from within the fire ring. He turned over several large bones that appeared to be leg bones and sifted through the pile, shifting ashes and bones out from the center. His stick struck something metallic. He stepped in closer and dug at the object with the stick. Ramirez moved in closer, leaning forward as he gained renewed interest in the activities of his partner.

Within minutes Wetzel had the metallic object separated and pushed out away from the pile of bones and ashes. Retrieving his canteen, he poured water over it and watched it hiss and emit steam.

"Son-of-a-bitch!" Ramirez scratched the back of his neck with his left hand, holding the rifle sling tight in the other hand. "Why ... it looks like a belt buckle."

Wetzel felt nauseous as he read, "Silver City Bull Riding Champ, 1951." He cleared his throat and finished his thought, "Mr. O'Brian was wearing that belt buckle the last time I saw him."

"Jeez—" began Ramirez. He swallowed hard. "They burned the body with the deer carcasses?"

Tipping his hat back with his thumb, Wetzel released all the air from his lungs and sighed. "Don, you need to get Hunt and his State Police forensics folks in here as soon as possible. Several of these unburned bones are bound to be human." He thought a moment, the hazel eyes narrowed. "I'll follow the sign on up the canyon. The killer's only an hour, if that, ahead of me."

"I dunno, Jack." Deputy Ramirez' brow furrowed into a frown.

Wetzel sighed again. "Don't have much of a choice, Don. Somebody's got to stay at the scene and protect the evidence till help arrives. That's within your purview, amigo. Not mine."

Wetzel tapped his shoulder and the dog, Pepper, appeared and sat near his dusty boots. "Besides trackin's what I do best." He held up a hand to stop the deputy from interrupting. "I'll take the portable radio after you call in. When I figger out where he's headed, you can move whoever you want in for the arrest."

Wetzel removed the .45 pistol from his pack. Ramirez watched him check the magazine, insert it, charge the weapon, and place the safety on, as he called in their position and what they had found to Steve Hunt with the New Mexico State Police.

Wetzel tucked the pistol in the belt at his back. Shouldering his backpack, he reached in his shirt pocket and withdrew a Lucky Strike cigarette from the pack. Lighting it, he drew smoke deep into his lungs then exhaled. He thought, *My God, Maggie's goin' to take this hard.* He heard Ramirez finishing his radio conversation with the State Police as he looked up in the direction of Granny Mountain and the steep, difficult hike ahead.

Handing him the radio, Ramirez said, "You be careful, Jack, and keep us informed."

Wetzel nodded. "There's a spring on up the canyon. They call it Rock Spring. I'd say someone has marijuana planted up there. Most likely they've been taking it out along the river and Sapillo Creek to Highway 25. You might have a deputy check for sign."

"It's a bit late in the year for harvesting," stated Ramirez.

"Maybeso. But our killer's here an' he's still tending something worth killing for."

"Yeah, you've got a point," replied a somber Ramirez as he watched Wetzel toss his cigarette into the pile of smoking ashes and turn to stride up the canyon with the old dog at his heels.

The canyon proved steep and rocky as it ascended toward Brushy Mountain, but it was easy to follow and indicated at least some travel in the past. For the most part, the killer kept to the numerous rocks when traversing the canyon, not leaving many tracks, but there were several along the way with other telling sign for the determined Wetzel to follow and know he was still following the size 10 vibram soled boots.

It was past mid-afternoon when Wetzel found what he was looking for—black irrigation pipes under the vegetation adjacent to the trail. Upon closer inspection, he saw the smaller feeder pipes leading to where marijuana plants had been harvested. He squatted on his heels behind a gambel oak tree, fear knotting his stomach. Clutching the cocked .45 pistol with the safety off in his right fist, he moved slowly forward to where he remembered the spring was located, the old dog in front of him. He closely monitored the dog's ears and overall demeanor to alert him of possible ambush. Knowing he was dealing with someone with bush skills similar to his own or even better, maybe a hunter or ex-military, he couldn't be too careful.

Wetzel found the spring without incident and slowly canvassed the entire area feeling more and more secure that the killer had left the area. He found an extensive network of plastic pipe coming from the spring and fanning out under the local vegetation to alleviate any possibility of sight from the air. He estimated there were possibly a thousand plants or more that had been harvested from the site.

He heard the helicopter long before he saw it, flying low over the river to the east headed to rendezvous with Deputy Ramirez. The killer would know something was up. What would he do? What the hell was he up here for anyhow? It appeared all the marijuana plants had been harvested and hauled out. He called Ramirez on the portable radio and advised of his findings and that the killer had continued north, then turned onto the Forest Service trail coming up from the river near the top of Granny Mountain, and was headed westerly along the ridge top. Wetzel memorized the boot print he followed in the dusty, maintained trail.

Large alligator juniper trees near the trail marked with the Forest Service heel and sole blaze provided unnecessary shade on a cool September day. Wetzel's woodsman stride carried him quickly along the old Forest Service Trail as he followed the easy sign. Grama grasses swayed in the breezes atop Granny Mountain as the piñon pine, gambel oak, and occasional Ponderosa Pine stood steady in the wind. Intermittent mountain mahogany bushes rustled in the occasional wind gusts. Then suddenly there were no more visible tracks in the trail.

Craggy Granite Peak and the Forest Service Lookout tower stood tall against a cloudless blue sky to the northwest. Brushy Mountain, where an old, tired "Bear" Moore had died many years ago on its snow covered slopes, lay to the north. Wetzel knew the trail junction about a half-mile distant lead either to Granite Peak itself or down into Turkey Creek in a westerly direction. He'd surmised the killer was headed for Turkey Creek then south to another marijuana field. The lack of sign in that direction baffled him and made him suspicious of ambush again.

Pistol in hand with the old dog close, he circled for sign where the tracks ended and easily found where the killer had abruptly dropped off the ridge on the northwest side of Granny Mountain headed straight down into the steep and treacherous Sycamore Canyon. Why in the hell would he do that? It made no sense at all, but the sign did not lie to Wetzel. It was hard as hell for a man to hide his sign while descending into steep territory. Would the killer take the canyon down to the river? If that had been his intent, he could've headed back to the river following the Forest Service trail from atop Granny Mountain.

As Wetzel tucked the pistol back in the belt against his back, he contemplated on what to do. He had only a few hours of daylight left and had no intention of tracking at night. Squatting on his heels, Wetzel rubbed Pepper's head; the old dog's eye lids closed momentarily, his tongue protruded as he gently panted enjoying his new master's attention.

"Wel-l-l ... Pepper ol' buddy, there's only one way to find out where this guy is headed." The old dog turned his gray head toward him, and waited for instructions. Wetzel narrowed his eyes as he peered down into the steep canyon. He murmured, "He's good, boy, an' I'm bettin' he knows we're after him."

The old dog stood slowly, carefully stretched his gaunt frame, shook himself and trotted down into the canyon with a surprised Wetzel scrambling to his feet to follow him down the steep incline.

It took the better part of an hour to traverse the steep canyon. The sun had set some time ago without the man or dog noticing; they stepped onto and around boulders and rocks to ascend the other side of Sycamore Canyon following obvious sign left for pursuers to follow. Wetzel kept the dog near him as he scanned the steep hillside they were ascending. As he labored up the incline he noticed the weather had warmed considerably from previous days; perspiration ran down his face and neck. Breathing hard, he stopped just beyond where the brush began and there were no large boulders or rocks to navigate around.

Peering intently up the hillside where the sign led, his sharp eyes saw nothing. No movement. No discernment of colors or shapes that seemed out of place in the landscape. He breathed a sigh of relief as he removed the pack from his sweaty back and lowered it to the ground beside him. It was then he noticed the old dog. Pepper leaned into the wind; his ears pointed up at attention, a low growl escaped his mouth. *Shit!* Wetzel forced his frozen body to react. As he dove to the ground reaching for the pistol, an arrow hissed overhead where his chest had been a second before.

Frantically, he gripped the pistol, pointing it uphill and pulled the trigger. Nothing happened. *Dammit!* He'd forgotten to release the safety. He did so quickly, re-positioning the pistol to fire. Pepper yipped loudly, and then whined shrilly as Wetzel saw he was impaled with an arrow that had entered his left side.

A flitting movement of camouflage appeared in the trees. He fired two rounds from the .45 pistol at the hillside above him as he grabbed the old dog and dragged him behind a nearby gambel oak tree. Chillingly, he saw the arrow shaft resembled the one left in the cottonwood tree at the murder scene. It had not exited completely as it had struck a rock on the far side. After several attempts to break the shaft, he finally did so, and then swiftly withdrew the bloody arrow from the old dog's torso.

Wetzel's mind clouded. To his horror, images that had been shut out from his memory for a long time suddenly appeared. Loud explosions, dying, disfigured soldiers, screams, the blood—so much blood. Then fear overwhelmed him. He struggled to erase the images, to send those skeletons back into the closet where he knew they belonged. *Not now, for God's sake.*

Trembling from the adrenalin rush, he tried to stop the

blood gushing from the dog's side. Pepper was hit behind his shoulder where the jagged wound indicated a lung and possibly heart pierced by the arrow. The old dog emitted a low whine, his tired eyes locked on his new-found friend's face. The eyes fluttered, the lids finally closed in death.

Wetzel lay there cradling his savior in his arms behind the oak tree. *Oh, my God. Pepper, I'm so sorry, boy*. Tears ran down his cheeks. His teeth clenched, eyes hardened as he held the old dog even closer. The large, dark shadow of Brushy Mountain loomed overhead then extended its tentacles down the rock-strewn slopes into the recesses of Sycamore Canyon. Night fell on the two friends.

CHAPTER TWENTY

McMurtry maneuvered his Game and Fish truck south along Silver Heights Boulevard and turned onto College Avenue headed west. Western New Mexico University beckoned to him from atop a high knoll further west. He slowed down as he neared the Gila National Forest Supervisor's Office, and parked the truck along the street in front of an old, white two-story house located across from the green government office complex.

Scratching his scruffy beard, he pondered on whether he should go inside or not. He wasn't afraid. It wasn't that atall. He was just wary of the dadjimmed hippy place. Ah, hell, he might just as well get it over with. Shrugging his massive shoulders, he stepped out of the truck and adjusted the yellow ball cap on his head, canting it just slightly to the right. Then placing his hands inside his worn, patched coveralls, he strode up the worn, cracked concrete sidewalk to a house that appeared extremely narrow in proportion to its height.

There he hesitated momentarily as he read the sign near the ornate glass door to the establishment, "Massages – A Far Out Experience". Rolling his eyes, he shook his head as he stepped up on the stoop porch and to the front door. He rang the door bell then waited impatiently for someone to come. The thought ran through his mind to leave, and he started to step off the porch.

But he didn't have long to wait. Soft footsteps sounded nearby, a shadowy figure appeared on the other side of the glass door; it opened, creaking on rusty hinges. A smiling face with lots of teeth answered the door. "May I help you? Mister—?"

McMurtry took his cap off hurriedly, grasping it in his big hands. "Well, ah ... McMurtry's mah name, ma'am."

A broad smile widened on the woman's face and her big, brown eyes smiled. Her long, dark hair was pulled tightly back on her head and trailed down her back to well beyond her thin waist. A fresh flower was tucked into her hair on the right side above her ear. She was wearing a white cotton blouse. Numerous beads of various bright colors adorned her neck and flat bosom. A beige cotton skirt flowed down from her waist to her ankles. The toes of her bare feet, nails painted red and green, protruded from under the skirt.

"Won't you come in, Mr. McMurtry?" She opened the door to its full width and stepped back to allow entry of the big man.

McMurtry shuffled his boots before answering, "Thank ya kindly, ma'am. Believe I will." He stepped into the interior of the house while grasping his cap and noticed a very small parlor with wooden floors; a mattress lay on the floor in one corner; the only furniture in sight. Directly in front of him, a steep, wooden stairway wound its way up to the second floor of the house.

As his eyes darted quickly around the room, he was unable to ascertain from where he stood if there were any other rooms adjacent to the parlor. Licking his lips, he said, "I ... uh ... understand y'all do ... uh—"

The woman's teeth were displayed again as she looked him over. "Massages?"

The sweet smell of incense quickly filled his nostrils. He thought maybe sweet for some but sickening pungent for one so used to the fresh smells of the clean air outdoors.

The Wildlife Officer showed his discomfort as he crushed his yellow cap tightly with both hands. The insignia "Tennessee Vols" on the cap cried out for him to cease.

"Yes, ma'am," he replied thickly.

Her soft brown eyes searched his bright blue eyes. "For ... yourself, Mr. McMurtry?"

As he stepped backward instinctively from those piercing inquisitive brown eyes, he damn near fell down as he tripped over his own feet. "*No!*" His short laugh had a quiver in it as he shook his burly head. "Not for *me*, ma'am. I ain't into them dadjimmed massages or sech goin's on."

The woman waited for him to continue; the smile was gone.

McMurtry looked furtively around the room. "What I mean to say, ma'am, is mah girlfriend—well, Juanita told me she'd like one o' them massages that y'all hippies do." He couldn't decide if he wanted to put his cap in a back pocket or hold it. The unruly, disheveled hair on his head pointed in all directions at once.

"So ... you would like to set an appointment for your girlfriend to have one ... *o' them dadjimmed massages*. Is that the short of it, Mr. McMurtry?" The brown eyes were smiling.

He stood unsteadily on his feet, glimpsed at the circling staircase, the mattress on the floor in the corner, and again for any possible adjoining room on the first floor. Finding none, he retorted, "Yep. I reckon that's about it, ma'am." Turning slightly to his left, he saw what he had been looking for—a small doorway behind the staircase. It was covered with long strings of several sized beads of various designs reaching to the floor.

The woman stated she needed to jot the necessary information down and would return momentarily. As she disappeared through the doorway of dangling beads clinking gently together, McMurtry noticed again the faint scent of incense and other unfamiliar scents from things he imagined hippies most likely concocted.

The woman returned, scheduled the appointment and accepted payment from the Wildlife Officer. She thanked him for the business and opened the door. A half-grin pulled at the corner of her mouth. "You're not from around here, are you, Mr. McMurtry?"

It was his turn to grin as he stepped onto the concrete porch stoop, placing his ball cap on his head. "Somehow, I've heard that before, ma'am." They both laughed loudly, and he said, "My friends call me, Mac."

"Well, Mac, my name's Naomi. And it's been a *real* pleasure meeting you."

***

McMurtry reached his parked truck, feeling mighty proud of himself for completing what he considered to be a very difficult task. Breathing in the fresh fall air, he opened the door and began to climb in when he heard a scream. Frowning, he listened intently. Another more muffled scream came from behind an abandoned house further down the street. A dog barked. He jumped in and drove his truck quickly down the street, sliding to a stop in front of the old dilapidated house.

Running quickly through the tall weeds and grass and around to the rear of the house, McMurtry observed a tall, good-looking blonde woman in a mini-skirt backed up against the side of the house and a large, powerful-looking man grasping her by the throat. The man wore a Silver City Police uniform and carried a sidearm. *What the hell?*

Still grasping her by the throat, the man pulled her toward him then slammed her head hard against the wall. He shouted, "You'll do as I say, damn you!"

McMurtry shouted, "Hey!" and lurched forward, still unsure what to do as it involved a police officer. It was then he noticed the little dog—a poodle—all dressed up with a cute hat on its head secured with a ribbon. The dog bit at the officer, growled, then bit him directly on the leg. The enraged officer shouted profanities at the little dog, who kept dodging kicks aimed in its direction without losing the tiny hat perched on its head.

The young woman pulled free from the grip on her throat and shouted, "Stop it! Joe, you stop ... right now." The policeman hit her square in the face, knocking her to the ground then turned on the dog and swung his leg back to kick it. His red face with bulging eyes turned toward McMurtry, who now stood beside him. The Wildlife Officer hit him hard in the face, knocking him to the ground. McMurtry reached down, retrieved the revolver from the officer's duty belt and placed it in a front pocket of the coveralls. He blurted out, "Just ... what the hell's goin'on here?"

The dazed officer struggled to get up. He weighed more than McMurtry, but wasn't as strong. He spat at the Wildlife Officer. "You stay the hell outta this, you goddamned country hick!"

Looking at the officer's name plate on his uniform shirt, McMurtry said dryly, "Well now, Officer Peach, that there is the *wrong* answer," and he hit him again this time on the point of the chin knocking him senseless. Quickly, he turned the stunned officer on his stomach and handcuffed him behind his back with handcuffs from the policeman's duty belt. He didn't bother to secure a key to double-lock the handcuffs.

The woman had retrieved the little poodle and stood leaning heavily against the building.

"You all right, ma'am?" rasped McMurtry as he searched for additional weapons, finding a .38 caliber revolver in an ankle holster. This he placed in a back pocket as he stood, breathing hard.

Her eyes wide with fright, she wiped blood from her mouth and nose with her trembling left hand while holding the poodle with her right. Looking at McMurtry, she nodded her head.

McMurtry said, "I'm a Game Warden with New Mexico Game and Fish Department, ma'am. Why did that officer hit ya?"

"I'd rather not discuss it, if you don't ... mind," she stammered.

McMurtry stepped closer. "I reckon ah *do* mind." He waved his hand sharply toward the handcuffed officer on the ground then in her direction and shouted, "I just beat the hell outta 'nother peace officer and arrested 'im after I watched *him* assault *you!*" He took a deep breath and lowered his voice. "Now, you're goin' to tell me why that is."

"He'll kill me if I talk," she replied.

"He ain't gonna kill nothin'. He's goin' to jail—now talk!"

Her pale blue eyes looked at him momentarily then looked down at the ground before she spoke. "I work for Millie." She looked up to see if he understood. "You know ... at the ... house over on Hudson Street," she said, "an' Joe's been extorting money from Millie for some time now. A lot of money. That an' takin' *me* for free whenever it pleases him."

McMurtry said nothing and made no judgments.

She licked bloodied lips and wiped at a bloody nose. "I told him today I wanted nothing more to do with him—"

The Wildlife Officer completed the sentence, "An' he

didn't cotton to that, did he?"

"No."

McMurtry pointed to the still unconscious police officer lying on the ground. "I'm goin' to the truck, ma'am, get my notepad and call for transport assistance from Grant County Sheriff's Office on the radio." His craggy face was hard. "If'n I ain't back an' he tries to git up, why, you turn that lil' ornery dog loose on 'im and holler at me, you heah?"

The woman nodded her head as she cradled the little poodle closer in her arms.

As he strode away, McMurtry muttered, "It ain't right, dadjimmit. Hittin' a woman. I don't care if'n he is a peace officer. The low-down, yeller sumbitch."

He was still muttering as he reached in his truck for the Game and Fish radio microphone. "Why, there's no call for it. None atall, an' fixin' to hurt that lil' dog, too!"

CHAPTER TWENTY-ONE

Wetzel clutched the .45 caliber pistol in his blood-crusted hand as he carefully snaked his way up toward Brushy Mountain following sign left by the assassin. It was a hot day for September, and he sweated profusely as he crawled amongst the dense shrubs and trees. However painstakingly slow, he had determined not to fall into a death trap again. His clothes had been drenched in the dog's blood and were encrusted. At first light he'd attempted to contact law enforcement authorities, but was unable to get out on the portable radio.

A mourning dove cooed high on the mountain. Wetzel recognized a ladder-backed woodpecker, an uncommon resident in the Gila wilderness, as it hammered away high on a dead limb of a gambel oak tree. He reckoned it was mid-morning due to the position of the sun in a blue, cloudless sky. It had become very hot, the sun blazing down on him as he worked his way up the south slope of Brushy Mountain. The dense vegetation provided excellent cover for the killer and had slowed Wetzel's movements considerably.

Upslope winds began to increase in velocity requiring Wetzel to shove his stained Stetson farther down on his head to keep from losing it. The more he questioned why the killer had chosen to travel to Brushy Mountain, the more it made no sense at all. To be sure there were Forest Service trails that traversed the north side of the mountain and led to the river as well as to Little Creek, and even

Turkey Creek, the destination he had initially envisioned the killer using. But as the saying went, it was the long way around the barn. Again, it made no sense to him.

Two things happened simultaneously. He heard Don Ramirez calling him on the portable radio, and he smelled smoke in the air.

Scrambling, he secured the radio from his pack and called the Deputy Sheriff. Noticing that he was now almost mid-slope, he heard Ramirez answer him, asking if he was all right.

"I'm okay, Don, but the dog's dead."

"What the hell happened?" Ramirez asked.

"He took an arrow meant for me." Wetzel reached up to further secure his hat in the wind.

Ramirez quickly responded on the radio, "We need to get you out of there, Jack. Is there a helispot up on Brushy Mountain somewhere we can use?"

"There is ... but I'm not sure where the killer is." Wetzel heard a helicopter approaching. Peering down slope from his position, he observed heavy smoke and flames below him. *What in the hell?*

Ramirez's strained voice broke his train of thought. "Where *are* you, Jack?"

"Maybe half-way up South Brushy from the river," he replied, the hazel eyes now concentrated solely on the conflagration of dense smoke and flames directly below his position.

The helicopter circled below him, disappearing momentarily from time to time in the thick, dense smoke. The Deputy Sheriff's radio transmission came across garbled and unreadable. Then, "... setting fire below ..."

Before Wetzel could respond, he heard the gunshots cracking out in the morning air. *A high powered rifle!* Then more rifle shots rang out. Wetzel could see the helicopter now. It was trying to gain elevation quickly.

"Jack! Some son-of-a-bitch is shooting at us! Break."

Again shots rang out.

Ramirez's excited voice, "We're hit!" Then: "The pilot's been hit! We're headed back to Gila Center if we can make it. Jack, get the hell outta there. *Now!*"

Wetzel murmured "10-4" but his mind was elsewhere. A chill ran up his back. *Had the killer circled around below him during the night while he slept?* Could he have done that? If so, Wetzel had a new found respect for his dangerous adversary. And where did he get the rifle? Did he have it with him and the bow as well ... or was there more than one assailant? His mind reverted back to the sign he'd been following. No, there had been only the one set of tracks. He was sure of it.

The small fire below him was gaining in size with several huge smoke columns billowing up into the sky, which was now rapidly turning gray. The fire, fueled by the strong winds, was taking advantage of the steep slope and continuous fuels. Wetzel shouldered his pack and quickly assessed there was no close safety zone to run for. The raging fire begun a strong run straight up the drainage where he stood; he was unsure of where to go for safety.

Turning his back to the fire below him, Wetzel jogged to the east hoping to get out of the chute and the serious danger it posed to him. After fifteen minutes or so, he hesitated in his flight and saw the fire had hooked well around his right flank and it was now running hard up the entire slope of South Brushy. He panicked, realizing he had no where to go to escape the raging inferno below him. Eyes wide, he just stood there watching Hell a thousand times over coming straight for him.

It was then, when in total despair and feeling a gut-wrenching fear, he heard the voice. At first, he thought he imagined it. Then again, the soft voice spoke, "Jackie. It's me, son."

A chill ran up Wetzel's spine. He peered upslope through the smoke and haze to where the voice had come. *Yes!* A hundred yards or so upslope from where he had stopped jogging, a man stood motionless, standing easy. He wore a battered, dull red fire helmet, the old style from the 1950s, a khaki long-sleeved shirt, and faded blue jeans. Who could it be? Keeping his eye on the man, Wetzel began running toward the tall figure. He stumbled over dead fall and rocks as he kept the man in sight.

Somewhat closer he recognized the bronzed face under the old fire helmet. *His father!* No, it wasn't possible. He stopped in stride and swallowed hard, his chest heaving from the exertion of running up the steep slope. No. *No!* It couldn't be ... his father had been dead since ... how long ago? Burned to death saving another firefighter on the Little Creek Fire in 1955.

The figure turned uphill, waving his arm. "This way, Jack. Hurry, son."

Wetzel stood, frozen in his tracks. "Dad?" he whispered.

The man turned and smiled. "We haven't much time, boy." The smile faded and a hard look replaced it. "You follow me, and you run hard!"

Wetzel ran past Murdock's Hole and sprinted straight uphill on upper South Brushy, the pack bouncing on his back. He fell, got up and fell again, but somehow managed to keep on running, his father just ahead of him. Smoke completely filled the air, burning his lungs and his eyes. He felt the intense heat from the billowing flames licking at his back. The searing heat burned his overworked, struggling lungs.

Tripping over a large deadfall, he fell headlong; the .45 pistol in his belt gouged his back. He struggled to his knees. The air was intensely hot. He couldn't breathe. Flames encompassed whole trees and a constant roar deafened his ears. *Dad! Please don't leave me.*

He stood, looking for his father, not knowing which way to run. A calm voice said, "Over here, Jack." Then through the dense smoke and searing flames, he saw his father again. A tall, good man, looking out for others just as Wetzel remembered him as a boy.

"I'm coming, Dad. *I'm coming!*" Wetzel willed himself to run. Made his failing lungs work, his rubbery, wasted legs perform when there was seemingly nothing left to give.

A large snag fell on his left as the conflagration raged all around him. Trees erupted in flames as he sprinted past, all the while behind his father on up through the South Brushy slopes to the summit of Brushy Mountain itself.

He lost sight of his father's broad back in the thick smoke then caught sight of him again. The whole world was as though in slow motion. Wetzel felt as though he was a spectator watching what was going on rather than being in the middle of an unforgiving inferno. An inferno that sapped his strength and every ounce of air from his failing lungs.

Still, somehow he ran. Much more slowly, but he followed his father to the crest and beyond. Then he fell heavily, rolled and came to rest against a large boulder that lay about fifty yards from the summit. Wetzel crawled behind the boulder. He dug down to mineral soil with his hands and placed his face next to the cool soil. Smoke permeated the air, but the intense heat was not present as it had been moments earlier. Gasping for air, he called out weakly for his father.

The fire continued to rage on the south side of Brushy Mountain, but had spent itself at the summit of the ridge. Wetzel called out again for his father. Nothing. Visibility was much better now, but he saw nothing of his Dad. He lay back on his stomach sucking in fresh air close to the ground. His lungs ached, his chest heaved. Fire talk crackled on the radio in his pack with Forest Service wild land fire personnel coordinating an attack on the demon that had been unleashed on an unusually hot, windy September morning.

Wetzel sat against the boulder still breathing heavily. With red-rimmed eyes, his blackened face looked from the north side of Brushy Mountain where he lay toward the large cut in the landscape which he knew to be Little Creek far below him. Then he scanned the vast, black, charred terrain to the west—thousands of acres that had been utterly consumed by the Little Creek Fire of 1955. And he did something he hadn't done for many years; he broke down and cried.

CHAPTER TWENTY-TWO

Ellen Wetzel was thoroughly enjoying the picture-perfect fall day at her small place nestled in the Mimbres Valley. Barely past forty-five years of living, she still could command a man's attention in her faded jeans, boots and a worn pull-over sweater. As she placed a steaming, hot cup of coffee in front of her son, she said, "Tell me what happened up on the mountain, Jack."

Wetzel quickly recounted what had transpired on Brushy Mountain. That the killer had escaped after the fire was set and hadn't been caught; the wildfire had been suppressed after the area was secured. Further, he spoke of his father appearing, calling to him and saving his life. As he spoke, his eyes brightened, his young, strong face beamed with admiration he felt for his Dad. Ellen said nothing, her sun-tanned face wrinkled at the corners of her eyes as she smiled at her son.

Wetzel hesitated. "Why? What is it, Mom?"

She sighed as she turned to pour herself a cup of coffee. "He ... called you ... Jackie?"

"Yes, he did," Wetzel said emphatically.

Sipping at the hot cup, she finally set it down on the kitchen table and sat down. "Well, I'm not surprised. He always called you that when you were a little button."

The room was still with neither mother nor son saying anything. The sunlight from a clear New Mexico fall day passed through the kitchen window, warming them as they sat quietly enjoying each other's company. Wetzel looked into his mother's eyes, the hazel eyes locked with hers. "He was there, Mom." Looking out the window, he murmured, "And he saved my life."

"I believe he did at that, son." She reached over and patted his hand. "You see ... I had a dream that day ... the day of the fire, and I heard him call to you." The smile returned to the pretty face. "And he *did* call you Jackie."

"*What?* Wetzel asked incredulously. Then: "How could he do that?" His brow furrowed, and he licked at dry lips. "How could he appear to me and to you at the same time, Mom?"

She said nothing for several moments, placing her elbows on the kitchen table and leaning forward. "Does it really matter *how*, Jackie?"

He sighed heavily. "No, I reckon not. What's important is that he was there for me, and I'll never forget it as long as I live."

"That's my boy!"

She thought of how much she missed her husband and best friend. How many times over the past sixteen years had she struggled, desperately living without him there at her side? Not a day went by that she did not grieve for his untimely death. In the aftermath of his death, she had asked why? Why had he felt compelled to go back into the fire after the missing firefighter? Even now, sometimes in a state of desperation, she asked, "*Why?*"

And the answer stared her square in the face. Because he was a good man who truly cared about others and felt it was his responsibility to help. She knew without a doubt that he couldn't have remained the man he was had he not tried to save another man's life that day so many years ago. But losing him had been so difficult for her, and at times, she lost her faith, felt sorry for herself and had even cursed

God for her misfortune. And she had many suitors interested in her over the years since her husband's death, but she found none the equivalent of her Tom. Even in the loneliness and desperation she had chosen to remain single.

Today, Ellen Wetzel blamed no one as she silently thanked God for allowing her son to escape the raging wildfire and live another day. A tear trickled down her cheek as she peered out the large kitchen window. Then she smiled and said to herself, "And thank you, Tom Wetzel, for being there for our son! One day ... I'll be seein' you."

Jack Wetzel stood, walked to his mother and encircled her with his arms. He hugged her and said softly, "I came home from Nam to find peace and quiet in these mountains. As of late, things have kinda gone to heck for me."

"I know, Jackie." She sighed. "I know."

CHAPTER TWENTY-THREE

Looking fierce some in the black New Mexico State Police uniform, Steve Hunt slammed his fist down hard on the desk. His face was livid as he stood facing the seated Silver City Police Chief Pete Thompson. "What the hell's going on, Pete?"

Thompson said nothing. His impassive poker face was impossible to read.

Hunt's voice was calmer. "I've got a murdered rancher whose body, by the way, was burned after he was killed by some crazy son-of-a-bitch with a bow and arrows." He shook his head and sighed deeply. "If that wasn't enough, the goddamned son-of-a-bitch tries to shoot down a Forest Service contracted helicopter with a sheriff's deputy inside. Then he sets a fire on Brushy Mountain and attempts to murder my tracker, Jack Wetzel!"

Chief Thompson stirred in his chair. "Sometimes life's a real bitch, Steve."

"Thanks, Pete," said Hunt facetiously.

Thompson leaned forward in his chair, elbows resting on the desk that was piled high with papers. "Just what do you want from me, Steve?"

"For starters, I want to know who your Internal Affairs Officer was investigating when he was murdered." Before Thompson could respond, Hunt continued, "*And* ... I want to know why one of your officers felt it was his unfettered duty to assault a woman right here in Silver City—in public no less, and in broad daylight!"

"You mean Millie's whore?"

"I don't give a good goddamn what she is, Pete. She didn't deserve that, and you damned well know it!"

Thompson picked at his teeth with a forefinger then looked out the dirty office window. "I'm gonna close that whorehouse down one o' these days."

Hunt leaned forward placing his hands on the desk. "I've got way too many corpses to investigate lately to worry about Millie's place, Pete." His hard brown eyes glared at Thompson. "Hell, Millie doesn't cause any problems; never has that I know of. Now, what can you tell me of your Internal Affairs investigation?"

"Officers were allegedly looking the other way, not arresting suspects in drug busts," said Thompson quietly out of the corner of his mouth, "and being paid to keep quiet on locations of marijuana grow sites and sellers around town."

Hunt sat down heavily in the chair. "Which officers?" When the Chief did not respond, he shouted, "*Who, goddammit?*"

Thompson's eyes flared momentarily at the State Policeman then were averted toward the floor. "The Lieutenant was murdered before he confided in me who was responsible."

Sighing heavily, Hunt rubbed his red face with both hands. He spoke with obvious control to his voice. "The file, Pete. Where's the IA file with all the information I need?"

Chief Thompson rose without responding and stood gazing out the dirty paned window again.

"Well?" Officer Hunt breathed loudly through an open mouth.

Thompson did not turn to answer. "Gone ... disappeared from the file drawer."

"You're shitting me."

Thompson turned. "No. Someone pried the locked drawer open and stole everything." He placed one hand on the other with his outside fingers drumming incessantly on the inside hand. Looking through the window again, he said almost absently, "There was a confidential informant the Lieutenant worked with ..."

Hunt stood abruptly. "Now, we're getting somewhere. Where's this informant?"

Silence, then: "Unfortunately ... he's dead, too. He was murdered the same night as the Lieutenant."

"*What?*" rasped Hunt.

The silence in the room was almost deafening. Thompson returned to his seat behind the desk. "You heard me."

Placing the palms of both hands on the desk, Hunt leaned forward. "Jeez, Pete. What the hell kind of officers do you have working for you?"

"Don't you get testy with me, Steve!"

"All right, dammit. Hell, you only have a handful of officers. Who's most likely ... say, in your opinion, to be involved in all this shit?"

"I'd say most likely, Joe Peach, but I don't have anything to back up my accusation."

Hunt was interested. "The officer who assaulted Millie's whore?"

"Yep. But he's on administrative leave pending trial."

"Give me his home address, Pete." The State Policeman's alert face betrayed a new found excitement. Receiving the written address, he headed toward the closed office door. Opening the door, he turned. "If Peach calls or comes by, you keep him here and call me, right away."

CHAPTER TWENTY-FOUR

It was a dark night; only a small sliver of a moon to illuminate the star-studded night sky. Market Street in Silver City was unusually quiet, traffic non-existent. The man stirred in the shadows of a large Chinese Elm tree. Dressed in black with a black ski mask covering his face, he was indiscernible to any possible passersby. His gaze focused on one of the small, faded blue single-story flat-roofed apartments located just west of St. Vincent de Paul Catholic Church. His right hand inadvertently moved in toward his darkened torso, the thumb and forefinger touching as if cupping a cigarette in the hand with the little finger nervously flicking at the ashes on the end of a cigarette that did not exist.

Another thirty minutes passed; the door opened on the apartment closest to the church. The dark figure melted back further into the shadows of the tree. A female voice resounded into the quiet night. "Robbie, stop playing with your toys and lock the door behind me." A slender, red-haired woman appeared at the door of the apartment wearing a denim jacket and carrying a purse. She hesitated before closing the door, repeated the order to the child and closed it securely.

The man watched closely as the young woman stepped lithely down the two steps onto the sidewalk leading to the church across the street. She ascended the steps and entered the church. Instantly, the man secured a pistol that was tucked in his back pocket and a silencer he now held in his left hand. As he walked stealthily across Market Street to the apartment, he attached the silencer into the muzzle of the semi-automatic pistol. Reaching the door of the apartment, he placed his black gloved hand on the door knob and turned it counter-clockwise. Beneath the ski mask his white teeth gleamed in the darkened night as the knob turned easily in his hand.

Opening the door, he slipped into the room noiselessly. A small boy about four years old lay on the floor playing with cowboy and Indian figures. As the man entered, the startled boy quizzically looked up at the intruding figure, but said nothing, his mouth open. Hearing the sound of dishes being handled in the kitchen, the man in black passed the boy with his finger against his lips then proceeded toward the kitchen. His right hand, which held the pistol, was now out in front of him supported by his left as he entered the small kitchen.

An elderly, slender woman turned from the kitchen sink holding a plate in one hand and a dish towel in the other. Gray shoulder-length hair fell into two braids, one over each shoulder. The dark, deep-set eyes widened as she saw him, the thin lips and mouth tightened in a shallow, wrinkled face, but she didn't drop the plate.

The man stood staring at the woman, the pistol lowered near his leg. His hard eyes fluttered under the ski mask. "*Yo la recuerdo, Doña Consuelo Vasquez,*" he said softly. "I remember you, *Doña Consuelo Vasquez.*"

The woman placed the plate carefully on the kitchen sink as she gazed calmly at the intruder.

"You killed my brother with your ... *veneno ...su pinche* poison, *y brujería* ...your damned witchcraft."

She said nothing, looking into the man's dark eyes that were clearly full of hatred. Her eyes hardened but showed no fear as she saw the pistol again come to bear on her. Placing both hands at her sides, she stood straight and tall in the small dimly-light room. Her voice was calm. "You're afraid of me? Of what *I* do?" She laughed. "I tried to protect your brother ... and *you* ... from the *brujo* you work for, *Tomás*. He ... his powers are what you should be afraid of ... not me."

The eyes of the man in black blazed at the old woman through the ski mask. "*Mentirosa*. Liar. He's *not* a witch! He's been like a father to me ... taught me everything I know."

The old woman's eyes narrowed. "And he's taught you *well*, *Tomás*. How to be a thief and a killer!" Contempt and disgust exuded from her voice.

"*Vete a la chingada, bruja,*" he murmured as he shot her twice in the head, "Go to hell, you damned witch."

She slipped to the floor without a sound. He bent and swiftly retrieved the empty shell casings then removed the silencer, placing the pistol in one back pocket the silencer in the other. He turned to the living room and the boy. He could see the boy had not witnessed the murder from his position on the floor. As he stood over him, the boy asked softly, "Who are you, mister?"

"A friend," the man said as he pondered what to do.

The boy stood. Soft, fine, brown hair covered his small head; two small brown eyes beneath long dark lashes peered at this stranger who had entered his home unexpectedly. The man detected no fear in the boy's eyes, only bewilderment at the ski-masked intruder. The boy wore a flannel shirt, and blue jeans covered the tops of worn tennis shoes. "I don't know you," the boy said emphatically. "Why do you have a mask?"

"Practicing for Halloween," the man said after a brief pause as he studied the boy.

The man made his decision. He motioned toward the door. "You need to come with me, Robbie. We haven't much time."

The boy backed up, clutching his cowboy and Indian toys in his fists. "My Momma told me to never go with strangers." His brow arched. "How do you know my name?"

"I told you. I'm a friend." The man shrugged. "Besides, your Momma told you to lock the door after her, too, didn't she?"

The boy hesitated as if feeling guilty. "How did you know that, mister?"

The man smiled. "I know everything, Robbie. Your Momma won't like that you didn't do what she asked, will she?"

The boy was quiet, contemplating what the man had said.

"You come with me." He shrugged again, "maybe I can get you off the hook. What do you say?"

Pursing his lips, the little boy put his hands on his hips. "I meant to lock it, mister. Honest Injun, I did."

The man's teeth gleamed under the ski mask. "I know that, Robbie. Come on. You an' me'll square it with her. Okay?"

He took the boy's jacket from a hook near the door. "Put this on, boy. Hurry!"

Hustling the boy out in front of him and closing the door, he peered both ways on the street to ensure there were no vehicles. He took the boy by the arm; they crossed Market Street and walked quickly around the corner where a pickup truck was parked. He placed the boy in the passenger seat, seat-belted him in, and locked the door. Returning to the driver's side, he got in and started the engine. He thought the stolen truck would serve him well tonight.

The little boy looked over at him. "Are you *really* my friend, mister?"

The man gazed at him as they drove away. His hard eyes softened slightly then hardened again under the ski mask. He didn't answer. Free from the steering wheel, the right hand cupped with the thumb and forefinger touching and the little finger seemingly flicked at the ashes of an invisible cigarette.

CHAPTERTWENTY-FIVE

Dressed in his official Forest Service uniform, Wetzel walked up the well-beaten path behind the Gila Visitor Center toward the helispot and living quarters. It was a beautiful fall day, the weather picture perfect. As he rubbed his square, tanned jaw, he was reminded he had forgotten to shave. He laughed at himself and adjusted the day pack more comfortably to his back. If forgetting to shave was the worst thing he did today, he'd be all right he reckoned.

Topping out on a small mesa above the visitor center, he saw the black New Mexico State Police helicopter sitting at the helispot, rotor blades spinning, and he had an instant flashback to Vietnam; he and his scout dog Smoky on their epic journey to Saigon. He thought of his old friend. *I hope you're at peace now, Smoky. I reckon I'm not quite there myself.* He sighed deeply, expelling the air from his lungs. *Maybe some day*.

Steve Hunt waved at him from out in front of the helicopter. There were two other New Mexico State Policemen standing nearby. They were all dressed in camouflage clothing and heavily armed. As Wetzel walked toward them, someone in a green Forest Service truck intercepted him near the housing area. District Ranger Bill Hood poked his large head out the window. His eyes squinted in the bright sunlight beneath heavy brown horn-rimmed glasses.

"I say there, Wetzel. I need a moment to visit with you."

Wetzel stepped up to the driver window. "Yes sir?"

District Ranger Hood used his right forefinger to push

the heavy glasses back up on the bridge of his large bulbous nose. Then he tilted his pointed chin down, peering over the newly adjusted lenses. In the bright morning light, his short-cut crew cut made him look almost bald. "I say ... I don't want you carrying a gun today. You hear me?" Before Wetzel could answer, he added, "Forest Service policy, son. Forest Service policy musn't be violated."

Wetzel's eyes betrayed nothing. "Yessir."

District Ranger Hood picked at his teeth with his tongue. "I heard you might've had a gun the day of the fire on Granny Mountain." He cleared his throat. "Won't do, son. Won't do ... can't—"

"—violate Forest Service policy," retorted Wetzel, "I understand, sir."

"Very well. Very well. I'm glad you understand. I'll fire any man who does so." Clearing his throat again, he added, "Got to have rules, you know." He peered over his glasses. "Are we clear on that?"

Wetzel licked his dry lips then let the air out of his lungs. "Yessir, very clear, sir."

District Ranger Hood straightened in the truck seat, attempted to put the truck in gear, and stripped the gears in doing so. He looked straight ahead. "I've work to do, Wetzel. Carry on with my orders." He drove away, the truck lurching in the wrong gear.

As Wetzel walked up to Steve Hunt, the New Mexico State Policeman swung his head toward the retreating Forest Service truck. "What the hell did *he* want?"

Wetzel grinned as he removed his day pack. "Nothin' much, Steve."

Hunt watched as Wetzel unzipped the pack and withdrew a Colt .45, Model 1911 pistol and stuck it in his belt behind his back. "Something about Forest Service employees not being authorized to carry firearms or some such thing."

"I see. Well, we wouldn't want you to violate policy and say ... *get killed*, now would we?"

Wetzel said nothing, closed the pack and slung it on his right shoulder.

They walked back to the other officers, and over the whine of the helicopter engine, Hunt said, "Let's go to Haystack Mountain and catch some dopers, boys." He nodded at Wetzel, "You ride up front with the pilot and lead us in."

***

Wetzel adjusted his headset for the intercom system over his green Forest Service baseball cap. The helicopter pretty much followed along the West Fork of the Gila River, passing White Creek Cabin to the north. Then off to Wetzel's right, prominent Mogollon Baldy stood majestic at 10,778 feet in elevation. He pressed the intercom button as he pointed directly ahead. "Steve, the drainage directly in front of us running perpendicular to our route of travel is the West Fork of Mogollon Creek. The next smaller canyon is Rain Creek, and Haystack Mountain is that high point up on the ridge just west of Rain Creek."

Hunt's voice crackled over the intercom. "Where can we land this thing?"

Wetzel pointed for the pilot's benefit as he spoke. "There's an old helispot near the top. See?"

The pilot nodded, heading for the landing zone.

Wetzel spoke over the intercom for everyone's benefit. "Haystack Spring is due south about a half mile from Haystack Mountain. There's another spring another half mile or so down that header into Rain Creek."

He pictured the terrain in his mind for a moment. "Foster Spring is due west of Haystack Mountain—about a half mile as well. If you get turned around as to where you are later on, just follow the drainage you're in down to Rain Creek and the forest boundary or from Foster Spring down Cherry or Minton Canyons to the boundary."

Hunt replied, "You and I'll go south, Jack. The other officers west," and then he spoke to the pilot, "Keep this bird flying for recon and commo, but keep it up high where the sons-a-bitches can't shoot at you."

"10-4," replied the pilot over the intercom, signaling an affirmative response.

The pilot landed the helicopter without incident at the old helispot, the officers jumped out with their packs and weapons then moved to a safe distance out in front of the helicopter. With every man accounted for, Hunt gave the pilot a thumb up sign and off it went to higher elevation and safety.

Weapons and packs secured, Hunt nodded to the other two New Mexico State Policemen, and they headed down off the ridge toward their pre-arranged destination, Foster Spring. Hunt turned and found Wetzel already moving south toward Haystack Spring. Cradling the shotgun in his arm, he followed suit.

Wetzel waited till he figured he was close to the spring then he pulled the pistol from his belt and flipped the safety off, his finger outside the trigger guard. He moved much more slowly and deliberately, using any cover and concealment available. The latest ambush attempt on his life was still vivid in his mind. According to reliable informants, there were several marijuana grow sites in and around both springs, all fed by plastic pipe and smaller feeder lines. The Grant County Sheriff's Office had officers stationed below them near the Forest boundary. Wetzel's friend, Deputy Don Ramirez, was in charge of the deputies waiting at the boundary. They had driven in part way, stashed their vehicles and hiked in via an old jeep trail the night before, the same route the drug smugglers allegedly used. The added bonus, according to the State Police informant, was the Silver City Police contact with the dopers would be on site. Wetzel thought, *yeah, right. Everyone is most likely running like hell down to the forest boundary after hearing the helicopter land up on the mountain.*

Just as Wetzel thought, Haystack Spring had adequate water and sure enough a black pipe extended from the spring downhill. As he descended warily through the thick brush with Hunt a few paces behind, he observed the smaller feeder lines leading to marijuana grow locations beneath numerous trees. From sign on the ground, Wetzel could see the illegal plants had been harvested recently. There were several footprints in the dry, sandy soil, but none appearing of the size or style of the man who had attempted to kill him previously.

Wetzel dropped over to the other header canyon that fed into Rain Creek and waited for Hunt to catch up. He pointed at recent sign on the well-beaten path. "We could have company up ahead, Steve." Taking his pack off, he withdrew his plastic water bottle and drank deeply.

Hunt did the same then whispered, "How much farther to the second spring?"

Wetzel shrugged. "Maybe a hundred yards ... maybe more."

They continued down the header drainage making little sound.

Wetzel saw the camouflaged man first. He was kneeling beneath a large juniper tree near a bundle of marijuana plants that had been neatly tied together for easy transport. Hunt leveled the shotgun at him while striding quickly toward him. “Throw your hands up!” he commanded, “or I’ll shoot!”

The man stood, turned slowly toward the advancing State Policeman. He raised his hands to shoulder height. Wetzel recognized him. Joe Peach! Wetzel raised his cocked pistol as his pulse intensified.

Peach grinned broadly, his large, ugly face creased into a smile. “Why, howdy there, Steve!” He peered up at the blue sky overhead. “That your helo up there?”

“Shut up!”

“I’m sure glad you showed up. I’ve been lookin’ for this marijuana site for awhile now.” His hands began to lower.

Hunt stood directly in front of him, the shotgun leveled chest high. “I said shut the hell up, Peach. You’re under arrest.”

“Sure, Steve. Whatever ya say, man,” Peach murmured, “but ... uh, what about them boys down yonder?” as he nodded his large head down the drainage.

Hunt took his eye from Peach for just a second, and the Silver City Policeman grabbed the shotgun barrel with both hands. The shotgun discharged, echoing up the canyon. Wetzel looked in horror as the two officers struggled for possession of the shotgun. He scrambled toward them, his pistol raised.

As Hunt and Peach wrestled for control of the shotgun now held high, Wetzel saw Peach reach down quickly with his left hand and place it into the camouflage jacket pocket. Then he pressed the pocket next to Hunt’s torso while he held onto the shotgun with his right hand. The report of a handgun startled Wetzel. He saw Hunt stagger back holding his stomach, losing control of the shotgun to Peach. As Peach turned toward him, Wetzel slid to a kneeling position and aimed at his old high school classmate. He yelled at the top of his lungs, "Drop it, Joe!

Peach grinned as he racked a round in the shotgun. "Come on, war hero! Come an' get some o' this, boy." He swung the shotgun up to his shoulder and fired.

Wetzel dove to his left as he fired the Colt .45. He felt the buckshot hit the ground near where he had knelt moments earlier. Continuing his roll to better cover behind an oak tree, he peered out from behind the tree with his pistol extended. Peach was gone, mostly likely running with the others toward the forest boundary.

Wetzel rose quickly and ran to the downed New Mexico State Police Officer. As he ran, he heard shooting below them.

CHAPTER TWENTY-SIX

Police Chief Pete Thompson awoke from a heavy slumber. He listened intently; a noise outside he was not familiar with? He looked at the alarm clock on his dresser. It was 2:30 a.m. *What the hell?* He heard it again. A scratching noise from the direction of his back porch. Fully alert, he slipped out from under the sheets without waking his wife who was enjoying a deep sleep. Reaching in the top dresser drawer, he pulled on soft leather gloves then withdrew a .38 caliber Smith & Wesson Model 60 two-inch revolver from the drawer and proceeded barefoot to the darkened living room dressed in his pajamas. Hesitating briefly before continuing to the kitchen toward the back door, he could literally hear his heart pounding in his chest. The absence of a moon made it impossible to see outside through the kitchen window.

Thompson took a deep breath, opened the door slightly and slipped out into the darkened night, his revolver extended. He moved to his right and stopped, allowing his eyes to adjust even further. Still he couldn't discern any shapes or forms that did not belong in his back yard. The huge cottonwood tree stood out even in the darkened night. The noise again! But where? Then he heard a low moan. *From where, dammit?*

Cautiously, Thompson made his way out slowly from the cement porch. He stopped in his tracks as he saw a form lying on the ground near the old cottonwood tree. As he aimed his revolver, his finger tightening on the trigger, he said, "Who are you? And what the hell are you doing in my backyard?"

The form stirred, a large bald head appeared out of the darkness. With difficulty, a man responded, "It's me, Pete. Joe Peach." And arm extended from the torso and the man moaned loudly. "I'm hurt badly, Pete." Another gasp as the form moved on the ground.

"What the hell happened to you?" Thompson asked. He knelt beside the camouflaged officer and saw blood covered the entire left shoulder and most of the policeman's chest.

The Police Chief repeated his question this time more sharply, "*What happened?*" He assisted the officer up to a sitting position against the tree.

"The State Police raided the marijuana sites below Haystack Mountain. I had to ... kill ... that State Policeman ... Hunt." Peach groaned holding his injured shoulder. "Wetzel guided them in—the son-of-a-bitch!"

"*You* killed Steve Hunt?" asked Thompson incredulously.

"I ... I ... think so. Shot him in the belly ... then tried for Wetzel ... missed. He got me with a lucky shot." Peach cried out in the night, "It hurts like hell, Pete!"

"You've ...*got* to help me". The wounded officer grabbed his superior and Thompson could smell Peach's blood now smeared on his own pajama top. "I'm most bled out ... can't walk ... anymore." His voice trailed off in the still star-studded night.

"Who knows you're here, Joe?"

Peach swallowed hard. "No one ... everyone else ... is ... dead."

"Everyone?"

"At Haystack." Peach struggled to speak. "Sheriff's deputies ... were ... waiting for us."

Thompson looked back at his quiet, darkened house. That his wife was still sleeping soundly he had no doubt. "We've got to get you some help, Joe." He patted Peach lightly on his right shoulder. "Are you armed?" he asked almost as if he did not care.

"Revolver ... in ..." Peach gasped as he swallowed with difficulty, "jacket ... pocket."

Thompson retrieved the weapon from Peach's pocket. He changed position near the officer, faced the house and fired two quick shots, both from the kneeling position that hit in the yard near his residence.

Peach struggled to sit up higher against the tree. "*What* ..."

He could see Thompson now faced him in the darkened night, and he heard the report of yet another firearm and the accompanying muzzle flash close in the stillness of the dark night. The burning pain began instantly, now in the center of his chest, emanating out. He struggled to speak as his large widened eyes displayed unimaginable fright and his sweating face total bewilderment.

He sank back against the cottonwood tree, tried to speak but could not as blood trickled from his mouth.

Thompson leaned in close almost touching the officer's face and whispered in an almost conciliatory tone of voice, "You're a liability for me now, Joe. Can't have you shooting off your mouth, now can I?" He straightened as he saw the light come on in the house. His wife called out to him as he reached out and felt for a carotid pulse on the mortally wounded officer. Finding no pulse, he placed Peach's discharged revolver in the officer's still right hand and stood, walking back toward the house, stopping briefly to tell his wife to call police dispatch. He himself moved to dispose of the gloves in the trash can.

CHAPTER TWENTY-SEVEN

It was approaching midnight when the man dressed in black turned the stolen truck onto the road leading to the Gila Cliff Dwellings off Highway 15. His teeth gleamed in the confines of the truck cab. The black stocking mask that covered his face was now rolled up on his face. No traffic; just as he had ascertained. He peered at the boy asleep in the passenger seat next to him. The man laughed under his breath. He knew they'd come after him now with the boy kidnapped from a murder scene. He passed Woody's Corral and slowed the truck as he neared the parking lot.

Maybe they'd send the same tracker as before? *Como chingan!* How they f... with me! He'd welcome the challenge, but his confidence told him no one, not even that guy could equal his skills in the woods and especially his ability as an assassin. He laughed again under his breath.

He parked the stolen truck. Not bothering to retrieve the keys in the ignition he got out, slammed the metal door hard, walked around the truck and retrieved his backpack from the bed. He slipped it over his shoulders, adjusted the straps then opened the passenger door. The boy sat upright only half awake.

"Get out!" the man's voice barked in the still, cool night air. It was a full moonlit night with twinkling stars in the sky.

The boy hesitated. The man grabbed him by the shirt front and dragged him out of the cab and onto the asphalt parking lot. "Damn you. When I tell you to do something, by God, you do it!"

Fully awake and frightened, the boy looked up at the man. His dark brown eyes under furrowed brows and long lashes indicated disbelief. He spoke with childlike softness to his voice, "Why are you treating me so rough, mister? I haven't done anything to you."

The man did not respond, but reached to his belt and withdrew a pistol, checked if it was loaded, reholstered it. He reached into the back of the truck to withdraw a large bow and arrows. These he placed over his shoulder.

The boy persisted. As he stood, he said emphatically, "I don't like you, mister." His little lips pursed as his big brown eyes began to well up. "You're a *bad* man. My Momma wouldn't want me to go with you." His lips trembled with fear.

The man's eyes gleamed within the dark mask as he stood over the little boy with his small hands on his hips. "You got guts, Robbie. I'll say that for you."

The little boy took a step back.

The man knelt with surprising quickness. He looked directly into the boy's eyes. "Here's the deal, boy. I don't give a damn what your mother wants. She don't mean shit to me." He pointed a forefinger at the boy. "You either come with me ... or ... I'll kill you where you stand." He waited for the words to sink in. "*¿Comprende?* You understand me?"

The man in black stood watching the boy's face turn from bewilderment to outright fright. He waved for the four-year old to walk in front of him. "Now *move*, and don't stop till I tell you to."

With tears silently wetting his cheeks, the little boy walked down the trail in his little tennis shoes toward the West Fork of the Gila River.

Once in the West Fork, the man made him stay in the

riparian area and the water as they passed the trail junctions to Little Bear Canyon and after another couple of miles, Woodland Park. The boy nearly stepped on a rattlesnake that was out hunting near the trail adjacent to the riverbed. He cried out loud then sobbed as he stumbled his way on into the darkened night, his wet tennis shoes squishing as he walked. The shadows of the huge Sycamore and cottonwood trees displayed intricate bizarre designs on the trail ahead as the light from a full moon filtered its way through the heavy tree canopies. A Great Horned owl hooted in the night and the man watched the boy jump in his tracks. Yet, not a peep out of the boy.

The gruff voice resounded in the quiet night, "Keep moving, boy."

The boy grudgingly complied with the order and mumbled, "You're *real mean*, mister. I'm going to tell my Momma on you."

They crossed the West Fork on several occasions following the trail. The boy had difficulty maintaining his balance on the smooth river rock. His tennis shoes and pants legs were water-logged, and he began shivering in the cool, fall air. Still, the man in black pushed and prodded him on into the dark night.

CHAPTER TWENTY-EIGHT

Wetzel arose early, grabbed a cup of coffee to take with him and drove his truck down to the Forest Service barn to feed the horses and burros in the corral. They were waiting for him. *Rosita* sauntered up to the gate with *Chochi* close behind as Wetzel brought part of a bale of alfalfa hay out to the adjacent corral. *Rosita* stuck her nose through the opening in the corral. As she brayed in the cool morning air, her long eye lashes fluttered at the master she had come to know.

"All right, girl. Here ya go." Wetzel laughed as he threw a flake of hay to her then to *Chochi* and his saddle horse, a buckskin gelding who trotted up to chase the burros away from their morning breakfast. Throwing another flake of hay to the sorrel gelding standing in the corner of the corral, Wetzel ensured all the animals were spaced far enough from each other so all could eat without interruption.

He heard a vehicle drive down the road toward the barn. A door slammed as he pulled himself up on the top rail of the corral and sat watching the animals feed noisily. Footsteps sounded on the barn's concrete floor then Don Ramirez appeared. Replete in the full uniform of a Grant County Deputy Sheriff with a .357 revolver strapped to his hip, Ramirez walked to where his friend sat on the corral.

"Howdy, Jack."

"Howdy yourself, Don." Wetzel's brow furrowed. "What you doin' up here at this hour of the morning, amigo?"

Ramirez leaned on the top rail, placing a booted foot

on the bottom rail. At first he said nothing. "It's turning out to be a busy day for me."

"Oh?" Wetzel turned his full attention to the deputy.

Sighing, Ramirez said, "A stolen truck was left in the Cliff Dwellings' parking lot last night."

Wetzel said nothing.

Tipping his straw hat back from his forehead, Ramirez continued, "We think it's the same truck that was used in the kidnapping of a young boy from Silver City."

Behind the barn the sunrise appeared in the east, casting an orange glow to the clear sky that was void of any clouds.

Wetzel leaned forward as he sat on the top rail of the pole corral. "Why in the hell would someone kidnap a boy and bring 'im all the way up here from town?"

Ramirez pulled his hat back down on his head shading his face from the sun. "Can't make any sense of it. I thought you might help us figger it out." He grinned. "That is if you're not too busy with the Forest Service an' all."

Wetzel rubbed his square jaw with his right hand. "Me busy?" He laughed aloud and shook his head. "I'm suspended from duty for carrying a firearm in violation of Forest Service policy. The District Ranger wants to fire me." He jumped off his perch to the ground. "And I don't have any idea when my hearing will be scheduled."

Ramirez's dark eyes softened. "I heard about that. I'm sorry." He looked down at the ground then directly at Wetzel. "You'll help me?"

It was Wetzel's turn to grin. "Bein's I got lots o' time, I reckon you got my undivided attention, amigo."

***

During the short trip from the barn to the trailhead, Wetzel was silent, thinking of all the possibilities why someone would bring a kidnapped boy up to the forest. He could not think of one logical reason.

Wetzel stepped out of the sheriff's car and walked up to the truck that was parked at the trailhead. Seeing nothing in the bed, he looked in the cab and saw a key in the ignition. Shaking his head, he peered at the trail just beyond the asphalt edge of the parking lot. A small tennis shoe imprint was clearly legible in the sandy soil. His interest peaked; his trained gaze continued up the trail and saw what he was looking for—a much larger boot print that was also clearly legible. Leaning forward, he looked more closely at the boot print. The skin prickled at the back of his neck, sending a shiver through his body. Instantly, he was absolutely certain the vibram print belonged to the killer he had tracked previously. The very same killer who had nearly ended his life not so long ago.

Wetzel turned to Deputy Ramirez, who now stood at his side. "The boy?"

"An old woman was murdered," Ramirez hooked his thumbs into his jeans pockets, "and the boy was taken."

"Judging from the tracks, I'd say the boy's not much older than four or five years." Wetzel looked up the trail, thoughts racing ahead from his memory of what lay beyond on the trail and possible destinations. Still, nothing made any sense to him.

Ramirez cleared his throat. "I ... ah ... the boy ... he's Maggie and Juan Garcia's boy, Jack"

"What?"

"The son-of-a-bitch took Robbie. And we have no idea why."

"*Jeez*. Maggie know about all this?"

"Only that the boy was taken."

"Better he's taken than murdered outright, Don."

A Game and Fish Department truck drove up and parked alongside the sheriff's car. A truck door opened and slammed shut. Officer McMurtry was out of uniform; as usual, his battered yellow ball cap tilted slightly to the right. His large frame ambled up to the other officers. He tucked his hands into the pockets of his brown coveralls. "Howdy, boys." He grinned broadly and breathed deeply of the cool air. "Fine mornin' ain't it?"

Wetzel grinned back. "How ya been, Mac?"

"Couldn't be any better, boys." He nodded to Ramirez. "How you fellers doin'?"

Turning from the edge of the asphalt parking lot and trailhead, Wetzel said, "We've got a killer who murdered a woman and kidnapped a boy." He shrugged and shook his head. "Then for whatever reason that same killer brought the boy out here last night and headed up the West Fork."

McMurtry's eyes brightened as he knelt at the trailhead, peering intently at the obvious sign left in the sandy soil. He spoke without looking up at Wetzel. "Size ten boot, I'd say. That feller walks mostly on the outside edge of his heels an' his left leg drags jest a mite." He scratched at his beard. "Maybe a war injury or some sech thang, boys."

Wetzel snorted. "I suppose you'll tell us how much change he has in his pockets, uh?"

Not hesitating, McMurtry stood. "A dollar an' a nickel. Four quarters and a nickel to be exact."

Ramirez chuckled. "Damn you're good, Mac."

"Damn good bullshitter, I'd say," said Wetzel.

McMurtry tucked his hands in his coveralls and spread his feet to a more comfortable stance. "I'm the master, Jack. Ain't nobody as good as me in trackin', son."

Ramirez' face became serious. "I asked both of you here to see if you two would track this killer and get the boy back."

Both men were silent, each into their own thoughts on the matter. Ramirez continued, "I've got a call at the Roberts Ranch to make—suspicious persons. I can be back by mid-afternoon to go with you guys."

Wetzel said, "The news this morning says it's supposed to rain by tonight."

McMurtry nodded, "It'd be best if Jack and I got on this within the hour. If it does rain, we'll have a helluva time tryin' to find any sign."

Ramirez looked at both men. "So you'll work it together?"

Both men nodded. The Deputy Sheriff breathed a sigh of relief.

"*Bueno*. You'll need a radio," he said as he tossed a handheld radio at Wetzel.

Wetzel looked at the radio. "Unless he climbs out of the West Fork, we might not be able to contact you by radio."

"Whenever you can, Jack. That's all I ask."

McMurtry started for his truck. "Best quit lollygaggin' and git to work, boys."

Wetzel winked at Ramirez. "The *master* calls, Don. We'll be see'n ya."

CHAPTER TWENTY-NINE

The crumpled letter grasped tightly in her trembling hand, Maggie Garcia sat on the edge of the bed. Her head bowed as tears flowed from her reddened eyes down her cheeks. She cried out, "My God, what's to become of me?" Her pursed lips trembled uncontrollably.

She knew she was feeling sorry for herself and she shouldn't do so, but somehow she just couldn't help herself. Coming home after praying at church, she'd found Doña Consuelo murdered, lying in a pool of blood in the kitchen and her son kidnapped. *Kidnapped!* The murder scene horrified her beyond belief, but the fact that her son had been taken brought unimaginable horror and grief to her.

Drying her tears on the back of her hands, she straightened the letter and peered at its contents once again. It was a letter from her husband, Juan Garcia, posted May 14, 1970:

Dearest Maggie,

I thought about not sending this letter to you as I know you do not comprehend what it is like here in Nam. Honestly, I'm not sure that I do. So many of my friends have died—so many that I have literally quit making friends any more.

I'm sitting alone in my tent. I feel lonely and afraid. Not so much for myself anymore, but for the others. The killing just goes on ... and on. I can't wait till my year is up, and I get the hell out of here like my friend Wetzel did. I live in a horrid world of death and violence with no escape. One of my friends was killed yesterday when we were on patrol. He hit a trip wire and a land mine bounced up at groin height, exploded, and blew his stomach, private parts, and legs apart. He didn't die right away, and I can still hear his screams ringing in my ears.

I have always done my duty and volunteered where others wouldn't or couldn't do their duty, but my dreams are fading and my outlook on life is so different now. I may live through this war, but I'll never be the same person who asked you to marry me in a time that seems so long ago. I just have to go on...like Coach used to tell us when football games were tough.

Will there be an ending to all this? If there is, I'm ready for it, whatever that entails.

I love you so much, Maggie, and lil' Robbie, too. I know you are taking good care of him. I look forward to seeing both of you soon.

Your loving husband,

Juan

"I lost you two years ago, Juan, and now ... I've *failed* to take good care of Robbie. I've failed you, Juan." Maggie's body shook uncontrollably and she cried out again. When the tears stopped she stood still trembling, leaving the letter on the bed, walked aimlessly into the empty living room and started out the front door of the apartment. The phone rang. She hesitated in the doorway, the phone continued to ring several times. Finally picking it up, she said nothing.

"Maggie?" The voice on the other end of the line was urgent.

No answer.

"Maggie, it's me, Don Ramirez."

Still no answer.

"Maggie, Jack Wetzel and the Game Warden from the Heart Bar are tracking your son in the Gila Wilderness."

Maggie's heartbeat quickened; she choked and couldn't

respond.

"Answer me, Maggie." Ramirez hesitated, then: "Jack said he'd find him—for you not to worry."

"Don … I … thank God for you and Jack." She had to get to the church and pray for those helping to find her son, her Robbie.

"I'll keep you informed, Maggie. You need anything, you call me. Everything will be all right."

Hearing nothing but sobbing on the other end of the line, Ramirez closed his eyes momentarily and hung up the phone.

CHAPTER THIRTY

It was dark and cold. The little boy's jacket was too light for the cold fall air. He shivered, waking up. His teeth chattered. He heard the water running into the river, and suddenly the urge to pee overwhelmed him. Afraid to move, he held his groin tightly with his hands as his eyes searched for the man in black. The man slept close by. The boy very slowly and quietly rose to his knees then to his feet. The man did not stir. *Momma, I don't know what to do. I'm so scared—of that man, the dark, and the woods.*

He could hear his heart thumping loudly in his little chest. His ears roared as he backed ever so carefully, away from where the man in black lay. In the water, the shadow of a dog appeared to him a short distance away. The little boy frowned, his eyes strained to see more clearly in the early morning light. The dog waited for him then turned, splashed up the river, turned and again waited patiently for the boy to come. As the boy neared the water, a voice whispered to him, *stay in the water, Robbie. It'll be harder for the bad man to find you if you stay in the water, son.*

"Daddy? Is that you?" the boy whispered in the stillness of the night. Silence.

He looked back from where he had come; he could no longer see the man lying on the ground. He turned and walked into the water, heading upstream toward the strange dog that waited patiently for him. He didn't know which direction he was headed—only away from the man he was so afraid of. He slipped on the rocks and fell headlong in the river, but he did not cry out. Getting up and keeping his balance, although with difficulty, he continued on in the cold water. Thoroughly soaked, the little boy shook uncontrollably, his teeth chattered continuously as he plodded on his hurried course away from the man in black. He had to get away from the bad man and not allow the man to catch him. And he had to find his Momma.

He cried as he walked, crying and sobbing intermittently. *Momma, where are you? What do I do, now? Oh, I'm so afraid. That man is so mean, Momma. I've got to get away from him and not let him find me*.

An owl hooted and he nearly fell again in the river. Frightened, he stood motionless in the running water that swirled around his legs, and his full bladder began to rid itself of its contents by its own volition. The scared little boy just stood there, cold and shivering, and wet his pants.

He thought he heard something behind him, and he turned and began walking hurriedly again always staying in the water and always away from the man in black. The dog disappeared from his sight.

CHAPTER THIRTY-ONE

As agreed upon, Wetzel took the north side of the West Fork and McMurtry the south side as they searched diligently for any sign to indicate the man and boy they now hunted had left the river. It was slow work, but Wetzel was pleasantly surprised at how quickly the Game Warden worked. For a big man, he moved quickly and obviously was a skilled tracker.

Wetzel watched him work the shoreline slowly and methodically, missing nothing before moving on up stream. McMurtry was dressed in camouflage except for his old yellow ball cap and a leather shoulder holster containing a .357 Ruger revolver. Like Wetzel he carried a light pack on his back for water, food, some extra clothes and a jacket.

Wetzel wore faded blue jeans, his White's boots, a denim work shirt, and his Stetson hat. The .45 Colt pistol Deputy Ramirez had given him was in the bottom of his pack; he carried a .30-.30 Winchester rifle that had belonged to his father slung over his shoulder.

Working in tandem, they reached the confluence of White Rocks Canyon and the West Fork, the same location where he and McMurtry had encountered the hippies months before. They rested briefly near the river and ate lunch McMurtry brought for both of them.

His mouth full, McMurtry said, "That Juanita ... she can make a heck of a boo-ree-toe, caint she?"

"You bet, Mac. She's a good woman." Wetzel swallowed a bite of his burrito with water from his canteen. "When are you'all getting married anyhow?"

"Juanita's ... thinking on it."

"Maybe you ought to get her boys to help in the decision process."

McMurtry smiled broadly. "Them boys are dandies, now ain't they?"

Wetzel took another bite out of his burrito, tasting the green chilis. "It's a shame we don't have time to make coffee."

McMurtry nodded, resting now on his elbows watching the river coursing by.

Wetzel felt talkative. "My dad told me when he was a young, recently hired ranger with the Forest Service, he met with his boss at a campsite near Lily Park one night. His boss was one of the old-timers who'd been hired as a ranger in the early 1900s during the infancy of the Forest Service. Anyhow, my dad was camped and his boss rides into camp about dark and says, 'You got any coffee?'"

Well, my dad's all embarrassed 'cause he don't have any. The old ranger swings down from his horse and just looks at dad like he's not hearing right. My dad had been working in the wilderness for a couple of weeks and was plumb outta coffee. Anyhow, he tells his boss he's outta coffee, but that he has some beef stew and he's welcome to a hot meal."

Wetzel grinned at McMurtry. "My dad said that old man didn't say a damn word; no sir, he just mounted his horse and rode off into the night." Laughing, Wetzel continued, "He never did come back to the camp."

McMurtry sat up, his interest peaked. "The hell ya say. Did he fire your old man?"

"Naw, he and Dad became good friends over the years."

"I'd be willin' to bet your old man had plenty o' coffee

for him the next time."

Wetzel laughed again. "He sure did, Mac."

A tassel-eared squirrel darted up the trunk of a large Ponderosa pine tree as a Cooper's hawk circled overhead. The sky had become inundated with clouds, a sign both men knew to indicate possible rain within hours.

Wetzel stood, stretched his lanky frame and placed his back pack over his shoulders as he watched McMurtry do the same. As he reached for the rifle, he said quietly, "This guy's a real bad one, Mac. He's very good in the woods, and he'll kill you without blinking an eye."

"Uh-huh."

"I should've had him the last time, Mac. If I had, he wouldn't have the boy now."

"Caint blame yourself, son. He's a slippery one fer sure. Most likely has some military background or some sech thang." McMurtry shrugged on his pack and headed upstream; Wetzel followed but on the opposite bank.

Working tirelessly, they were careful to watch for an ambush and to not miss sign showing either the boy or man they were pursuing had left the West Fork. Then without warning, Wetzel found their quarry's camp from the previous night. After whistling low at the Game Warden, he unslung his rifle and knelt near where the man and boy had slept. McMurtry came splashing through the water to his location.

They both reviewed the sign, and it was McMurtry who whistled low. "I'll be dadjimmed, that lil' boy plumb scooted outta here while that bad *hombre* slept." He laughed as he walked out around the foot sign, following both sets of tracks to the river. Wetzel's heart pounded in his chest. He saw McMurtry check for any sign at the mouth of White Rocks Canyon.

"Think he'll kill the boy when he catches him, Mac?"

The Game Warden thought carefully before he spoke. "Maybe he ain't caught him yet, Jack." They looked at each other and quickly began their search along both sides of the river.

It was Wetzel who caught the subtle sign left by the man with the size ten vibram-soled boots leading off from the West Fork on the north side into a steep side canyon. He whistled at the Game Warden as he stood looking up at the steep rocky terrain that jutted out of the riverbed. Why leave the river here? There were canyons ahead that were a lot less steep and rugged, some with trails. The man would make obvious sign as he worked hard at climbing out. Wetzel searched intently for the boy's tracks and found nothing.

McMurtry now stood beside him, the rushing water of the West Fork thrashing at his wet camouflage pants. He, too, looked for the boy's sign then up into the rugged canyon to the north. He almost whispered, "Where in the hell is he headed anyhow?"

Tipping his hat back on his head, Wetzel replied, "It's hard to say, but most likely Woodland Park." He was silent for a moment. "Maybe to set an ambush farther up, Mac."

McMurtry grinned, his blue eyes bright. "You an' me, why, we're thinkin' the same, son."

Frowning, Wetzel peered upstream. "You thinking the boy got away?"

"Yup." The Game Warden waved a hand upstream. "Still goin' thataway, I'd say."

Wetzel's hazel eyes locked with the blue eyes of the Game Warden from Tennessee. "You find the boy, Mac, and I'll catch the kidnapper." As he started toward the canyon, he felt a strong hand on his shoulder. The .30-.30 Winchester was removed from Wetzel's shoulder.

"I reckon not, Jack." McMurtry grinned again and scratched his beard, his blue eyes twinkled. "Bein's I'm the *master* at trackin', this here sumbitch belongs to me. I've not tracked anybody as good as him in a spell." As he peered up the canyon his eyes squinted and the lines around his eyes wrinkled, displaying crow's feet. He slung the rifle over his shoulder. The clouds overhead darkened the sky and thunder rolled in the far distance.

"You go find thet boy, Jack, an' take him home to his momma." McMurtry's voice had a metallic ring to it, "An' I'll find this here killer sumbitch." With that he was gone, the big man moving lightly up the steep canyon and was soon lost in the thick vegetation.

CHAPTER THIRTY-TWO

Wetzel hurried as much as he dared; he knew he was running out of time. Darkness would overcome him soon and the black skies were rumbling ever louder by the minute. The canyon walls were very steep now. He didn't think the boy would be able to climb out, but he didn't want to bypass him hiding somewhere near the river. The boy had to be frightened beyond belief, alone, wet and cold.

An hour had elapsed since he and McMurtry had parted ways. If he didn't find the boy soon, he'd have to stop for the night. He began having difficulty reading sign as the ambient light diminished. *Please, God. Help me find Robbie. Please!* A tremor shot through his body. On the south side of the river, he observed a flat rock that was maybe two feet from the river. Was it wet or his imagination? No, it was wet and others as well.

The wet tracks led to a large Sycamore tree then disappeared. A willow thicket was located nearby. The boy had to be close. *What should I do? Call out?*

Wetzel stood under the giant Sycamore tree and pondered his options. It was almost dark. No rain, but it was coming and he knew it. He made his decision. Taking his pack off, he leaned the rifle against the tree. Quickly, he found dry kindling and wood and built a fire under the sweeping branches of the big tree. Kneeling down, he gently blew into the fire; it came to life with bright yellow flames and crackling sounds. He added larger wood, a little at a time, and soon had a roaring blaze going among the rocks. Next he tied one end of his poncho to the tree and secured the other end with two stakes he made and drove into the ground. *I reckon the tree canopy and the poncho ought to keep us dry*.

He warmed his hands next to the fire as he squatted on his heels facing the willow thicket. Talking slowly but loud enough to be heard several feet away, he said, "My name's Wetzel, Robbie. I'm a *friend*. I'm not here to hurt ya."

He saw no movement within the thicket. His heart pounded in his chest. He wanted badly to charge the thicket, find the boy, and bring him next to the fire. But he knew better. *Patience, Jack ...patience, dammit*. Not moving, he said much louder, "I'm here to *help* you, Robbie—to take you back to your momma."

Still no movement.

Wetzel reached slowly in his pack and withdrew an extra shirt then a box of fire C-rations. "I have some fruit cake and a can of beans, son. Why don't you come over to the fire ... warm up ... then eat some food, uh?"

No movement in the willow thicket.

Nightfall had overtaken the canyon bottom of the West Fork. Lightning flashed across the sky followed within seconds with booming thunder.

Wetzel detected slight movement within the thicket. A boy's voice was barely audible over the thunder. "Mister ... Wetzel ... you're not ... friends with that bad man, are you?"

Wetzel's tanned face wrinkled into a grin as he squatted before the fire, trying not to move and scare the boy away. "No, Robbie. I'm one of the good guys, son."

No response. He waited several moments before he said, "Come to the fire, Robbie. Let's get you warm and dry before the storm hits."

Nothing.

Wetzel sighed deeply. Lightning flashed and the thunder rolled almost simultaneously. He heard a whimper then the little boy cried out, "I don't ... know ... *what* to do, mister!" He heard the little boy crying, and his heart went out to him.

Not moving, Wetzel waited a moment. "I can't decide for you. You think with your heart, boy. Do what your momma would want you to do."

The little boy appeared tentatively at the edge of the willow thicket. He was shaking and shivering from the cold and wet. Soaked from head to toe, he just stood there looking at Wetzel unsure of what to do.

"Might just as well come on over and warm up—get something to eat."

"There's a ... *bad* man out there ... try ... ing to hurt me."

Wetzel stood slowly. "I know all about it, Robbie. Your momma sent me to find you and take you home."

"But ... the bad man—?"

"I won't let him harm you." Wetzel gestured with his hand. "Come to the fire, son."

"He ... shouldn't be so *mean*, Mister Wetzel."

"No. I reckon not, Robbie."

"My momma ... she ... wouldn't like him," the boy said emphatically.

The little boy hesitated then moved slowly, stumbling toward the fire. Wetzel recognized hypothermia had already set in.

When the boy stood across the fire from him, Wetzel was cautious not to approach him too quickly. "You cold?"

"Yes ... sir." The boy shook badly. It was pitch black; the wind began to blow, whistling as it pulled hard at the Sycamore tree canopy and Wetzel's Stetson. A flash of lightning lit up the sky and thunder reverberated in the canyon. Wetzel smelled the aroma of moisture in the fresh mountain air.

Wetzel tossed his flannel shirt over to him. "You take off those wet clothes and put that shirt on. I'll warm up these beans and see if we can dry your clothes before the rain comes, uh?"

A rifle shot sounded high up near the rim of the canyon. Wetzel stood, unconsciously touching the .45 Colt pistol in his belt at his back. His hazel eyes met with the little boy's dark brown eyes across the flickering camp fire.

CHAPTER THIRTY-THREE

McMurtry stood behind an oak tree on the downhill side of the steep slope, his hands on his knees, breathing deeply, his chest heaving. *Dadjimmed country's steep! Have to keep going ... it'll be dark soon ... an' rain like hell.* He gazed through the foliage of the tree as he rested. The obvious tracks lead straight up out of the canyon bottom. The sumbitch wasn't trying to hide anything. Of course it would be difficult at best due to the steepness of the terrain not to leave sign, but—McMurtry was suspicious by nature, and somewhere in his gut he knew the man he pursued would attempt an ambush. Somewhere near the top?

Peering again through the foliage, he figured he was maybe halfway out of the canyon bottom. He placed his hands on his knees again. His thoughts raced back to the past, a time when as a young Game Warden in eastern Tennessee he had attempted to arrest a poacher hunting bear out of season. He'd not waited long enough behind the huge white oak tree before confronting the violator. *I was way too antsy in them younger years.*

The man had seen him from forty yards distance, turned and ran. McMurtry pursued him, but the distance was just too great with the poacher fleet of foot. The Game Warden lost sight of his quarry then he would catch a glance of him through the trees just ahead. For quite some time the two men raced through the hardwood forest.

Finally, McMurtry tired, his heart beat furiously in his chest, and his lungs burned for air. He stopped about mid-slope then as he had now, his hands on his knees, breathing deeply. Eventually, after regaining his wind, he looked upslope for his quarry and was surprised to find him resting on his own knees just above him about the same distance as they were from each other at the initial encounter.

McMurtry stood upright that day and hollered, "You 'bout rested up, son?" He saw the man's surprised face and bewildered look; then a smile appeared, and the poacher replied, "Whenever you're ready." They began the chase again, but time got the best of the Game Warden. Darkness overcame him, and he had to terminate the chase.

Just like today, dajimmit! Darkness would be on him soon. He looked up at the sky overhead. Dark billowing clouds added to his concerns of rainfall that would obliterate the tracks and sign he needed to pursue this ... killer ... this kidnapper sumbitch.

Sighing deeply, he formulated his plan quickly in his mind, drank water from his canteen then began a lateral movement from his rest location. He felt like a dadjimmed billy goat, stepping from rock to rock, and hanging onto trees, shrubs and rocks to assist in standing upright and making little or no sound. Then there was the concern of losing his footing and falling.

He came to a granite rock shelf, skirted around it and started up hill only to be startled by a buzzing, coiled rattlesnake a few yards away in the shelter of the rock outcropping. Moving stealthily along, using whatever cover he could find, he progressed slowly up the steep hillside.

The Ponderosa pine trees were more numerous near the canyon rim. Despite the cool breezes brought on by the storm, McMurtry wiped at perspiration running down his face, the salt burning his eyes. He crawled on his belly for about a hundred yards after removing his yellow ball cap and stuffing it inside his shirt. It seemed like a damn mile. Periodically, he stopped and listened intently. The clouds were mostly black overhead, lightning lit up the darkened sky and thunder rolled in the distance.

Cautiously, he inched forward on his belly in his camouflage gear. He grinned. Been quiet as one o' them church mice, now ain't I? Pulling himself up and over the rim, he rolled over on his belly onto a bed of soft pine needles beneath two large pine trees. He lay still for several minutes, peering to the west of his location, knowing the sign of his quarry led to that portion of the canyon rim.

He saw nothing. No movement.

The lightning and thunder had increased in the evening sky. McMurtry knew about where he would set up an ambush if he were the one being pursued, but he saw nothing out of the ordinary. He lay still, knowing his adversary had skills equal to or better than his own. D*on't doubt yourself, Mac. You're the master, son.*

Night began to fall on the canyon rim, but the Game Warden did not move from his location. His strained eyes began to ache from his meticulous searching for a quarry that had eluded him and all his efforts thus far.

A large bolt of lightning suddenly flashed across the blackened sky and within a half second thunder boomed loudly. The closeness of the strike startled McMurtry and his widened eyes discerned subtle movement from behind one of the large pine trees approximately a hundred yards west of his position. *What the ...?* Then nothing. He focused his full gaze on the site that was etched in his mind. His heart pounded in his chest; the adrenalin rush pulsated through his body as he lay still on the carpet of pine needles covering the forest floor.

Minutes passed that seemed like an eternity to him.

Still, he saw no further movement. Maybe he'd imagined it? Should he move toward where he thought he had seen something? It would be nightfall shortly. He didn't have much time left in the day. But something in his gut told him to stay put and to not move.

Another flash of lightning, and he saw what he had been searching for—a man dressed in black clothes standing upright behind the largest Ponderosa pine! McMurtry eased his rifle slowly along the ground out in front of him. The man in black shouldered his bow and turned to leave.

Now! Hoping Wetzel's rifle shot straight, McMurtry shouldered the rifle and peered through the open sights; he cocked the hammer back and his finger tightened on the trigger. The man in black hesitated briefly seemingly unsure of what to do, turned and looked down into the vicinity of the West Fork.

The sound of the rifle being discharged reverberated throughout the darkened night and within the steep canyon walls. *I outfoxed ya! Ya sumbitch!* Then thunder boomed loudly, roaring its displeasure in the black skies. McMurtry levered another shell into the chamber and knelt behind the tree. Lightning flashed, and his eyes focused again on where his quarry had been just moments before. Nothing. No movement. No sound. No shapes discerned to be out of place in the natural setting.

McMurtry felt strongly he had hit his target, but had he? It was almost dark. Time had run out for him. He took a deep breath and stepped out from behind the tree, crouching as he did so. Suddenly, something thudded into the tree near his head. Dropping instantly to the ground, he heard two more distinct impacts into the tree within seconds of each other. He rolled to his right and behind another large tree. His heart pounded furiously again in his chest.

Lightning flashed and lit up the sky once again. McMurtry looked at the pine tree to his left and to his horror; he saw three arrows imbedded in the tree, one below the other about a foot apart. *Jeez!* He swallowed hard not sure of what to do next. It was pitch black now and he could see absolutely nothing as he lay clutching the rifle. It began to rain then it poured, raining hard and steady.

CHAPTER THIRTY-FOUR

It rained steadily during the night with the sky occasionally opening up and the rain pounding the Game Warden who lay huddled under a large pine tree. Darkness faded to the gray of dawn and cloudy skies persisted with no precipitation. Still McMurtry lay quietly, listening for any sound to alert him of the presence of his quarry, who now may have turned hunter.

Not until McMurtry felt satisfied that the man in black had gone did he sit up and lean against the tree. Only then did he release the cocked hammer on the lever-action rifle, leaving a round loaded in the chamber. The day showed full light in the dark, overcast skies.

He stood, rifle at the ready, and slowly approached the location a hundred yards distant where his quarry had been the previous night. As McMurtry figured, the man in black was not there. *Most likely hauled butt and made use of the rain all night to cover his tracks.* It was what McMurtry would have done himself had the roles been reversed.

He searched to no avail for any sign that he had actually hit the man the previous night when he shot at him. No sign of blood or any other indication the man was hurt or injured. Removing his pack, McMurtry retrieved a Forest Service map and determined he was west of Grave Canyon. If he continued north a couple of miles, he should reach the Middle Fork of the Gila River and could take it down to Gila Center. That was if he didn't find the killer up here somewhere first. *I sure hope Wetzel found that kid.* He thought of his friend Juanita and her two boys.

Realizing he needed to concentrate on the dangerous task at hand, he shook off thoughts of the kids and headed north, walking softly on the pine-needled forest floor. Traveling about a half mile, he saw an old grave site marked by a pile of rocks and a dilapidated wooden cross near the head of Grave Canyon. Just beyond, he crossed a well-maintained Forest Service Trail that headed east and west. It was here on the north side of the trail he knew his quarry was alive and well. The sign was subtle, almost invisible, but the Game Warden's trained eye saw where someone used a branch to brush out tracks near the trail after crossing headed north. *I've got you now, you sumbitch.* He felt elated, almost giddy.

From that point on, he followed marginal sign or merely guessed as to where his adversary might travel. He came to another Forest Service trail and stopped short in his tracks. Clearly, in front of him on the trail were muddied tracks of a size ten vibram-soled boot. The tracks led down the trail a short ways to a trail junction where an official sign indicated one could either continue westerly to Prior Cabin or drop off the ridge into the Middle Fork of the Gila River to the Meadows.

The man in black had chosen the Meadows. As McMurtry followed suit, it began to rain steadily again. Lightning crackled in the dark skies and thunder resonated in the distance.

The trail down into the Meadows soon displayed numerous switchbacks and downhill steep grade. McMurtry thought to himself the grade was considerably more than the Forest Service standard of six percent. If a man rode horse back down this trail, he'd best tighten his cinch before descending into the canyon or he'd be hanging onto the horse's ears by the time he reached the bottom. The rain continued a steady down pour as McMurtry worked hard at staying on his feet in the mud and steep terrain. By the time he donned his green army poncho, he was completely soaked and didn't have a dry stitch of clothing.

He lost all semblance of sign of his quarry as he descended. Water cascaded down portions of the steep trail, running over and around logs or wooden water bars that had been placed in the trail by the Forest Service to contain erosion.

Finally, he saw he was about a quarter mile from the canyon bottom; muddied water flowed in the Middle Fork of the Gila River. The area immediately below him contained a short meadow full of tall green grasses bent over from the intense rainfall. McMurtry squatted down on his heels in the trail and surveyed the Meadows area thoroughly from east to west. He rested his eyes for a few moments then surveyed it all over again, this time more thoroughly. Nothing. No movement of anything or anyone.

Cautiously, he descended the remainder of the Forest Service trail to the Meadows. He skirted around the edge of the entire meadow his rifle cocked and at the ready, but he saw nothing—no one, not even an animal stirred as he strode through the vegetation surrounding the meadow. When he was completely satisfied it was safe, he walked to a large cottonwood tree near the Middle Fork and stepped under it. The huge canopy created an "umbrella" for some protection from the incessant rain. Chilled to the bone, his hands shook as he found some dry kindling under the massive tree and built a fire with some difficulty.

He knew if he intended to pursue the killer, best him when he did catch up to him, he would need rest and dry clothing. Breaking dead branches from the tree beneath its canopy, he was able to increase the size of his fire to where it warmed him and somewhat dried his clothes as he ate jerky from his pack. The afternoon became evening. The rain began again, pounded mercilessly down on the tree he had chosen for shelter. Darkness came and the rain ceased, but McMurtry did not realize it. He was fast asleep under the massive cottonwood tree where many a weary traveler, Indian and Anglo alike, had slept over hundreds of years. Even in his slumber, he clutched the rifle tightly in his hands.

A majestic bull elk with a large rack atop his head appeared tentatively on the eastern edge of the Meadows. He stopped momentarily as he stared in the direction of the old cottonwood tree, but he was upwind from the Game Warden and proceeded gracefully out into the lush grasses of the meadow and began to eat hungrily.

CHAPTER THIRTY-FIVE

The next morning Wetzel hiked out of the West Fork drainage at White Rocks Canyon via the Forest Service trail to a high point so he could talk and be heard on the Grant County Sheriff's portable radio. There he advised dispatch he had found Robbie O'Brian and that the boy was unharmed. He apprised them of the rifle shot he'd heard from the previous evening, knowing McMurtry pursued the killer. Further, he had no other information in regard to the incident involving the Game Warden.

The little boy stayed constantly at Wetzel's side and insisted on hiking the steep trail out to call on the radio when Wetzel suggested he remain in the West Fork drainage under the shelter of a large tree. The Sheriff's Office advised they would contact the boy's mother and transport her out to the Gila Cliff Dwellings parking lot.

Wetzel and the boy returned to the West Fork. The rain continued steadily, and they crouched under the protection of a sycamore tree to allow the storm to subside. Sitting next to Wetzel, the boy stared off into space. Eventually, he scooted closer, resting his head on the Ranger's shoulder.

Procuring a Lucky Strike cigarette from the pack in his shirt pocket, Wetzel stuck it in the corner of his mouth and lit it with his silver lighter; drawing the smoke deeply into his lungs he exhaled, the gray smoke exiting his nostrils to drift in the cool breeze that had picked up as they sat quietly near the river bank.

It was the boy who spoke first. "Mr. Wetzel ..."

"Call me Jack, Robbie. Please."

"Yessir. Do you think ... I mean, well, will my momma be mad at me?"

The question caught Wetzel off guard. The cigarette glowed as he drew on it, pondering; the cigarette danced along his lips from one side to the other then hesitated in the middle just dangling there precariously. "No, Robbie. I reckon not."

The little boy stood, his small feet soaking wet in his tennis shoes. He looked like a little drowned mouse to Wetzel. His round face, red from being out in the elements, showed seriousness to Wetzel. Robbie placed both hands on his hips and looked squarely at Wetzel. Frowning, he said emphatically, "I reckon you're wrong, Jack. She'll be plumb hopping, mad I'd say."

Wetzel returned the gaze, grinned as he took the cigarette from his lips with his left hand and flicked at the ashes with his little finger. He looked at the cigarette and flicked again, removing the remaining ashes from the end. "Naw, she won't, son. She's goin' to be tickled to have you back safe with her again."

The boy peered intently at him, his brows knitted. "That bad man ... he flicked his hand ... like you just did, Jack. But he didn't have a cigarette."

Wetzel was all ears. Kneeling close to the boy, he asked, "Did he smoke, Robbie?"

"No sir."

"But, I thought—?"

The boy thought more about what had been said then: "No, he never smoked—just acted like he really *did* have a cigarette in his hand and was flicking at the ashes."

"Uh-huh."

"I don't want to talk about him anymore, okay, Jack?"

"Just one more question, Robbie." Wetzel saw the rain was lessening as they talked. "Tell me, when you ran away from the bad man that night, how did you know which way to go?"

The little boy put his hands on his hips. His face became serious again as he concentrated on his thoughts. "There was a dog." His little round face smiled, the breeze pulled at his disheveled dark brown hair. "The dog ... he showed me the way."

Wetzel stood and dropped his unfinished cigarette to the ground. "What did this dog look like, Robbie?"

"Oh, he was black ... mostly, and ... brown," Robbie bit at his lower lip as he touched his own eyebrows, "and he had brown eye brows, Jack."

Kneeling before the boy, Wetzel felt his pulse quickening. "This dog. Did he run off?"

Robbie laughed. "Oh, no. He was only in my dreams; I think he wasn't *real*."

Wetzel sat back on his heels. His face clearly showed the shock of the revelation before him. "I knew a dog like that once."

The little boy's face became pensive. "Did he show you the way, Jack?"

"Yes. He surely did that, Robbie." Wetzel sighed deeply. "On numerous occasions, son. And just like he did with you, he saved my life, too."

"He was a good friend, huh, Jack?"

Wetzel's eyes saddened; a lump rose in his throat; he forced it back. "He was the ... best friend a man could ever have." He stood and patted the boy on his head. "Come on, son. Let's get you back to your momma."

"Okay, Jack. I still think she'll be madder'n all get out."

"You just remember you did nothing wrong, Robbie. It

was the bad man who was wrong, not you."

"Yes sir."

"Good boy. Now, let's move out. We've got some miles to hike."

As they started down the West Fork trail, the little boy reached up and took Wetzel's hand. He looked down at the boy, who was intent on hiking as fast as he could, and smiled. He thought, *if I had a son, I'd want him to be like Robbie. What a fine little fella you got here, Maggie.*

They hiked along for a time, the boy and man each in their own thoughts and neither one spoke. It was enough to enjoy the wilderness in each other's company. The rain ceased and the sun peeked through the least threatening clouds, appeared for awhile before it disappeared then reappeared moments later. Reaching the trail junction to Woodland Park, Wetzel sat on a rock, took off his pack and placed his jacket inside after procuring his canteen. He offered the canteen to Robbie as the boy scrambled up on the rock next to him.

Robbie drank thirstily, water running down his chin and onto his already wet shirt. Wetzel laughed as the boy handed the canteen back to him. "We're 'bout a mile out from the Cliff Dwellings. Might just as well rest a tad before we head in."

"I went to the Cliff Dwellings once with my Mom."

"Oh?"

The boy's face became pensive again. "I don't know how in the heck those Indians hauled water up to their houses so high up from the river."

Wetzel thought about what the boy said. From what he remembered about the cliff dwellers, they had built approximately forty rooms inside the natural caves and alcoves high above the canyon floor most likely for protection. They were a part of the Mogollon culture and lived only a short time at the dwellings. Building their structures with mortar, rock, and timbers from trees cut between 1276 and 1287 A.D., these pre-historic Indians forged a suitable subsistence on the abundant game and crops of corn, beans and squash from the rich, fertile soil of the Gila River valley until about 1300 A.D..

Wetzel cocked his hat back on his head with his thumb. He said nothing, knowing the boy had more to say.

"Anyhow, I would worry about stepping on a snake and breaking the water jug on the way up." He shook his head and pursed his lips as he looked at the older man sitting next to him. "I ... I wouldn't make a very good Injun, would I, Jack?"

Wetzel almost laughed then saw the sincerity on the little boy's face. He said solemnly, "If I was an Indian living at the dwellings, I can't think of anybody in the whole world I'd want with me more than you, Robbie."

The little boy's eyes brightened. "You wouldn't spoof me now, would ya, Jack?"

"I reckon not." Wetzel laughed as he pulled his hat down on his head and helped the boy down off the rock. They started down the trail and the boy took Wetzel's hand again. He looked up at the older man and smiled. "Jack Wetzel, I'm *glad* you're my friend."

CHAPTER THIRTY-SIX

McMurtry was up early before first light, ate the rest of his jerky and swallowed it down with water from his canteen. Slinging the rifle over his shoulder, he headed down the Middle Fork of the Gila River. He had lost all sign of the killer in the heavy rainfall and figured he'd just as likely headed that direction as any other.

Two hours passed as the Game Warden hiked steadily down the Forest Service trail that lay adjacent to the river. Heading eastward, he passed through very steep portions of the canyon that were heavily wooded. Large towering Ponderosa pine trees stood watch over the yellow and red-leaved cottonwood, sycamore, hackberry, and box elder trees; thick willows and emory oak added to the beauty of the riparian area. Rock spires standing alone extended up toward the sky that was clearing with patches of blue appearing periodically.

He emerged from the tall timber into a small meadow on the north side of the river and walked through a thick stand of brilliantly yellow sunflowers, towering above his head. Enjoying his hike and the country, he nearly missed the trail junction sign advising him to turn south via Little Bear Canyon enroute to the Cliff Dwellings some three miles distant.

Pulling on the pack straps, he adjusted the pack higher on his wet, tired back. As he turned to proceed up Little Bear Canyon, he hesitated. There in the trail, he plainly saw a partial vibram boot print in the sandy soil. He stepped close, squatting on his heels as he unslung the rifle from his shoulder. There was no mistaking the imprint of a vibram toe from a hiking boot. Quickly, he looked for other prints, but could not find any legible vibram-soled prints. *Is it the killer's track?* It was difficult to make that call with a partial print, but McMurtry decided to take no chances.

Cocking the hammer on the rifle, he moved stealthily along, observing occasional fresh sign headed north up out of the river bottom toward Jordan Mesa. No sole prints, but broken branches, disturbed vegetation. It was difficult climbing out of the canyon, and he was breathing hard when he topped out. He knelt down behind a piñon pine tree; the mesa was covered in thick stands of alligator juniper and piñon pine trees with a sprinkling of oak trees.

McMurtry smelled the faint odor of smoke in the air, determined the direction of the wind and walked cautiously in that direction. After traveling about a quarter of a mile, he saw a tent through the thick vegetation. His heart pounding, he held the rifle at the ready as he approached the camp hidden deep on top of the mesa.

He dropped to his knee with the rifle butt against his shoulder. A man was resting in a hammock slung between two juniper trees. A rifle leaned against the tree where his head lay. The man was dressed in camouflage. A small campfire smoldered nearby. McMurtry watched the tent for several minutes to see if there were other occupants. Seeing none, he moved to better cover behind a juniper tree about fifty yards from the sleeping man in the hammock; he could still see the tent clearly if anyone should exit.

His voice rang out in the stillness of the wilderness, "*You*, in the hammock! Throw your hands up!"

The man jerked upright, looking around frantically to

see where the voice was coming from; he reached for the rifle.

McMurtry leveled the rifle at his chest. "Touch that dadjimmed rifle, an' I'll kill ya, son."

The man's hand hesitated near his rifle.

"I'm a Game and Fish Officer. You're under arrest for kidnapping and murder. Put them hands in the air. *Now!* Damn you."

The man complied as he stood. McMurtry moved from cover and quickly walked up to within ten yards of the man in camouflage, covering him with the rifle. The man was dirty, unshaven with several days of beard stubble on his face and hair to his shoulders. His swarthy complexion was accentuated by his small black eyes set close together.

He spoke with a Spanish accent, "What's this all about?"

McMurtry motioned him to the ground with the rifle. "Shut up. On your belly. Git on the ground."

The man started to speak, "What—?

The Game Warden stepped in swiftly and knocked the man to the ground with the rifle butt. He rolled the man in camouflage over and placed handcuffs on his wrists behind his back and double locked them. Roughly, he grabbed the prisoner by his hair and belt and jerked him to his feet. Shoving him toward the tent, he asked, "Who's in the tent?"

The man spit blood and mumbled, "No ... body,"

McMurtry shoved him to the ground and aimed the rifle at the tent. Cautiously, he opened the flap. No one. The inside was littered with camp gear, clothes, a sleeping bag, and standing in one corner was a hunting bow.

McMurtry thought of the kidnapped boy. "Where's them black clothes you been wearin'?"

The man frowned, spit blood. "What ... black clothes?"

"Don't lie to me, you ..." McMurtry slapped him hard

in the face.

Struggling to speak, the man coughed, spat blood. "I ain't got no black ... clothes. I ... I just got outta the Army ... back from Nam. I ain't bothering ... nobody up here."

"The hell ya say." McMurtry shoved him back to the ground, looking at the man's feet judging the size then peered at the vibram-soled hunting boots next to the hammock.

"Like I was sayin', you're under arrest. You so much as twitch or cause a problem for me takin' you outta here, I'll bust you wide open." He grasped the man tightly by the shirt front and hauled him up to within inches of his own face. With clenched teeth, he rasped, "We *clear* on that, son?"

The man in camouflage said nothing, his small black, hate-filled eyes burned holes into the Game Warden's blue eyes; he nodded his shaggy head.

CHAPTER THIRTY-SEVEN

Wetzel swung his old truck into the Silver City Police Station parking lot off Hudson Street. Sitting close to him was the little boy, Robbie O'Brian, and his mother was riding shotgun near the passenger door. He parked and shut off the ignition. It was Wetzel's favorite time of the year—late fall with cool weather and for the most part clear, blue skies.

As usual, Robbie spoke first, "I'm kinda scared, Jack."

Wetzel looked across the seat at Maggie O'Brian sitting next to the passenger window. Her pretty green eyes showed concern, but she said nothing. She was the most beautiful woman he'd ever seen.

She said, "Jack, I appreciate all you've done for my son. I ... we can't thank you enough."

Pretty and really nice, he thought.

He smiled at her then twisted in his seat turning his gaze to the little boy, sitting between them. "Nothin' to it, Robbie. I'll be right there with you and your momma. Like I told you, the police will have some men in another room. All you have to do is look at 'em and point out the man who kidnapped you, if you can."

"I don't want to be near that ... bad man again, Jack."

Wetzel took the boy gently by the shoulders. "He can't hurt you anymore, Robbie. He's behind bars." He continued softly, "If you can identify him in the lineup, they'll lock him away for good. Okay?"

The little boy pursed his lips. "Okay, Jack." He looked

up at Wetzel and smiled. "We're burning daylight out here, huh?"

Wetzel laughed. "I reckon so, son."

The three entered the crowded police station. New Mexico State Police Officer Steve Hunt greeted them first as he stepped forward with outstretched hand to Wetzel. Grinning, he said, "My belly still smarts a bit, Jack, but I'm back at work." Wetzel noticed no heavy gun belt around his waist.

"I'm glad you're doing well, Steve. Is the lineup all set for Robbie? He's a tad nervous 'bout this whole affair."

Hunt turned to the little boy and knelt gingerly in front of him. "No need to be nervous, son. We just want to know if any of the men in the next room is the same man who kidnapped you. That's all." He stood and ushered all three of them into an adjacent small room then closed the door.

A large, heavy-set man in a Silver City Police uniform sat at a table. His voice was deep and gruff when he spoke. "Bring the boy up here by me, Steve."

Beyond the window in another room, two police officers were lining four men up against a wall. Robbie walked up to the window with Officer Hunt; he looked intently at the four men, a frown on his face. The gruff policeman said, "I'm Chief Thompson. I want you to look very closely at all these men then tell me if any of them is the man who kidnapped you, okay?"

"Yes sir." The boy peered through the window as he tentatively placed his small hands on the window sill.

"They can't see you, Robbie. This is a one-way mirror," said Officer Hunt.

Wetzel saw all four men were dressed in camouflage clothing. All appeared scruffy with long unkempt hair and unshaven faces.

The boy turned to Chief Thompson. "I ... I don't know. The man was wearing black clothes and a black mask."

The police officers had the men turn first to one side then a full 180 degrees back to facing the boy. An intercom was turned on and each was asked to repeat the phrase, "Get into the truck!" When that was accomplished, Chief Thompson asked impatiently, "Well, did you recognize the kidnapper's voice?"

Robbie looked at the men again for several minutes while the chief drummed his fingers on the desk. "No," he answered, "but the bad man's voice sounded kinda like the man on the end." He pointed to his left.

Thompson stood from his chair, pointed at the man. "That one ... the Mexican?"

"Yes sir, but I'm not sure that's him."

"What the hell do ya mean, you don't know? You were with him for some time," growled Thompson.

"If he doesn't know, he doesn't know, Pete," interposed Wetzel. "Lay off him."

Thompson turned on Wetzel. "Who the hell pulled your chain?"

Hunt stepped between the two men. "Now, hold on here. There's no need to get at each other's throats." He paused before speaking, "Robbie, are you saying you don't recognize the kidnapper in that room?"

The little boy started to cry. "It was so dark ... he had a mask."

"It's all right, son." Hunt motioned for Wetzel to take the boy out into the main foyer.

***

After Wetzel the boy and his mother had left; Officer Hunt closed the door and turned to Chief Thompson. "What the hell was *that* all about?"

"*Well?* He pretty much pointed to the Mexican didn't he?"

"He said the man *sounded* like him, but he couldn't identify him as the *one*."

"Good enough for me. Besides he's the one the Game Warden arrested with the bow."

"True enough, but I'm not sure how circumstantial evidence alone will hold up in court."

"We've made plenty of cases on circumstantial evidence over the years."

It was Hunt's turn to drum the fingers of his left hand on his right arm. "The suspect says he never kidnapped or murdered anybody, and McMurtry never found any black clothing or arrows for the bow."

Thompson grunted. "Hell, they all say they're innocent. He most likely burned the clothes and buried the arrows."

"Maybeso, Pete." The State Policeman turned and peered out the dirty window. He spoke over his shoulder. "You ever hear of a man who goes by the name of *Tomás*?"

The Police Chief's fingers drummed nervously on the desk for several moments. His eyes flicked toward the State Policeman's back then to the floor. "No ... can't say that I have." He cleared his throat. "Why, what's this ... uh, Tomás got to do with anything?"

Hunt turned to face Thompson. "Maybe nothing—maybe everything." Searching the Police Chief's eyes, he continued, "My buddy with the DEA in El Paso says an informant of his talks of a man by the name of *Tomás*, who comes and goes as he pleases from Mexico." Thompson's eyelids shuttered briefly.

"Word is that such a man, if he even exists, might be operating here in New Mexico working for one of the drug bosses down in Mexico."

Thompson's eyelids fluttered again. "Sounds like a ghost story to me, Steve." He chose to look at his fingers drumming on the desk top and not at the State Policeman.

"My DEA friend says this ... ghost ... is ex-Mexican Marine Special Forces." Hunt's voice had a metallic ring to it as he said, "If such a man were operating here in Silver City, I find it hard to believe *you* wouldn't be aware of it."

Thompson slammed his fist on the desk, his eyes blazed. "You believe whatever the hell you want. I don't give a damn."

Hunt placed his palms on the desk; his eyes locked with the Police Chief's eyes. "You'd better give a damn. In case you haven't noticed, we've got dead bodies stacked up here like cord wood—a rancher murdered in the forest, an old woman murdered right here in town along with your Internal Affairs Officer for Christ's sake! Then there's the assault on my tracker and Sheriff's deputies, a little boy kidnapped, your shootout with one of your own officers! Jeez, Pete, what the hell does it take to light a fire under you, anyhow?"

Thompson sighed. "You've got your man, Steve. He's sitting in jail at the courthouse."

"Maybeso." Doubt showed in Hunt's weary eyes as he strode to the door.

"You—uh, keep me informed of any new developments, huh?" The door closed; Chief Thompson sat at the desk deep into his own thoughts, his fingers drummed nervously on the desk top.

CHAPTERTHIRTY-EIGHT

Wetzel sat quietly watching District Ranger Hood shuffle papers in his lap at the Gila National Forest Supervisor's Office located east of the VFW hall in Silver City, New Mexico. He shared the room with Hood, a Human Resources employee for the U.S. Forest Service, and the Forest Supervisor himself, Warren Carter.

Carter was a self-made man who had worked his way up in the Forest Service ranks over a period of many years. Most of his service had occurred in the Southwest. He was a solid-built man with a barrel chest, and thinning, short gray hair that had been thick and dark in his younger years. Proud to be in the ranks of the U.S. Forest Service, he always wore his tan uniform shirt, green jeans and a pair of cowboy boots with pride. Carter was well respected by the Gila National Forest staff and within the Silver City community as a fair man who was very knowledgeable as a natural resource manager and leader.

Wetzel sat with his Stetson hat in hand and listened as his boss District Ranger Hood articulated how he, Wetzel, had violated Forest Service policy on several occasions, and after he had been clearly advised not to ever again carry a firearm while performing his duties as the General District Assistant for the Wilderness District.

District Ranger Hood's thick dark-rimmed glasses slid down the bridge of his large red bulbous nose where they skidded to a halt. His high pitched voice droned on about how this employee had been insubordinate in the regard of carrying a firearm on duty. He stated that he could not allow any employee under his supervision to violate policy.

Wetzel thought his short crew hair cut looked especially official this morning. Hood was about to lose a lower button on his uniform shirt where his protruding belly attempted to escape confinement above his belt buckle.

When Hood finished with his assessment of the facts in the case, Carter leaned back in his chair and rubbed his tanned jaw without speaking. Eventually, he turned his gaze to Wetzel. A quick, easy smile appeared then was gone. "Well, well, Jack. How the hell are you?"

Wetzel stirred in his chair gripping his Stetson. "Fine, sir."

"How's your mom?"

"She's doing well, Mr. Carter. Still ranching and enjoying it."

"Great woman—Helen Wetzel." He paused watching Ranger Hood's face turn redder as he discussed matters other than the hearing itself. "I knew your dad quite well, Jack. He was a fine man and an exemplary Forest Ranger."

Embarrassed, Wetzel pulled at his hat brim. "Well ... thank you, sir."

Carter continued, "I worked for him when I first started in my career with the government. Did you know that?"

District Ranger Hood interposed, "Sir ... with all due respect—"

Carter locked eyes with Hood until the latter dropped his gaze. "Hood, you've had time to tell your side of this. Now it's time to let others talk and for you to keep your mouth shut."

"Yes sir," District Ranger Hood mumbled.

Carter leaned forward with his elbows on the desk. "Now then ... this matter of the firearms; what do you have to say, Jack?" His brown eyes beneath shaggy gray brows searched Wetzel's eyes. The old Ranger's eyes displayed openness, an interest in hearing another's side of the events that had transpired.

Wetzel took a deep breath, exhaled and began, "Don Ramirez asked—"

Carter stood suddenly. "Let's see if I understand the facts, son." Turning, he peered out the large window in his office as he spoke over his shoulder, "You were asked by the New Mexico State Police to find a missing rancher, and after *voluntarily* agreeing to do so, the very man who murdered the rancher came very close to killing you." He turned back to face Wetzel. "Hood, here," he said as he motioned toward Wetzel's supervisor, "alleges you had a firearm with you when tracking this ... criminal."

Wetzel started to speak, but Carter raised a hand to silence him. "I spoke with the deputy who accompanied you on the search, and he stated when he offered a firearm to you for protection, you told him you had enough killing in Viet Nam." Carter sat in the desk chair his dark blue eyes blazed at Wetzel. "Is that accounting correct so far, son?"

"Well, yes ... but—"

"Yes or no?"

Wetzel exhaled. "Yes."

Carter turned to District Ranger Hood. "And, since we have no other corroborating eye witness stating to the contrary, I find the allegation for the first violation of forest rules in regard to possessing a firearm unsubstantiated and therefore dismissed."

Hood's face reddened, but he said nothing.

Leaning back in his office chair, Carter continued, "As to the second allegation, I understand you took a pistol with you when assisting the New Mexico State Police in their raid on the marijuana garden below Haystack Mountain." He grinned. "No real point in attempting to deny that as the bullet that killed Officer Peach came from your pistol ... and, after all, you were there, on forest property."

Wetzel started to reply; Carter again held up his hand. "Lastly, the third allegation. When you assisted the Grant County Sheriff's Office to search for the O'Brian boy who was kidnapped, Hood says you took a pistol *and* a rifle with you." He interlaced his hands as his elbows rested on the desk. "I spoke with Wildlife Officer Bob McMurtry yesterday in regard to the third allegation, and he very succinctly told me that if I was so ... *dadjimmed* interested in what my Forest Service employees took with them when they *voluntarily* tracked dangerous criminals, I ought to've been there, done the job and saved myself all the worry."

Chuckling, Carter said, "Then he proceeded to tell me he didn't recollect what the hell you had with you or what you were wearing during the search incident. He obviously had more important considerations."

Carter slapped his desk with his hands. "So, that leaves us with one out of three, now doesn't it, Jack?"

Wetzel said nothing.

Motioning toward District Ranger Hood, Carter said quietly, "He wants your head on a platter, boy." Pausing, Carter scratched the back of his head. "Fired. Terminated for insubordination."

Wetzel sighed, but again knew better than to speak.

"We have Forest policy in regard to prohibiting the possession of firearms while performing official duties for a couple of reasons: the most obvious is liability for the agency and secondarily to keep our employees out of harm's way. The problem today is that we actually put our employees smack dab in harm's way by sending them into dangerous situations without proper training or equipment, such as firearms, when raiding a marijuana field."

Carter stood again and turned to peer out the window. "We're going to rectify that situation soon by having Forest Service Law Enforcement Officers on the districts that are trained and armed for that type duty. It may take a few years, but by God, we'll make it happen. The Special Agents assigned in the regional offices just aren't available for the work load we have in the forests." His brow furrowed, he said softly, "I'd think a man with your skills and temperament would make an excellent Law Enforcement Officer for us, Jack."

Hood attempted to speak, "Warren, I hardly think—"

Turning abruptly, Carter said, "I haven't finished," as he pointed a finger first at Hood then at Wetzel. "That being said, Jack, you had no right to take a firearm with you on duty when your supervisor advised you not to do so against said Forest Service policy." Carter strode to the other side of the room then back.

He stood in front of Wetzel with his hands in his pants pockets. "It's for that reason that I've decided to suspend you for fifteen days, son. Since I figger the Forest Service caused half the problem, we'll split the thirty days I would normally suspend you." He nodded at the Human Resource specialist. "That's *without* pay, the suspension to take place forthwith." He gazed individually at each person in the room. "Do I make myself clear?"

No one dared speak. "Good! I consider this matter closed. Show yourselves out; I've got work to do."

CHAPTER THIRTY-NINE
November, 1972

McMurtry eased his Game and Fish truck in parallel with Little Walnut Road next to an older one-story house. The night was cold; Thanksgiving was just around the corner and the hint of snow was in the air. As he exited the vehicle, he pulled his brown canvas jacket out and put it on over his coveralls.

Juanita had invited him to a party at her *tia's* home, and although he welcomed the opportunity to see her and the boys again, he wasn't too sure about the family event or the aunt. Striding to the door, he could hear Mexican music playing and loud voices of folks having a good time. He stepped up on the porch and knocked on the door. No one answered. Knocking several times more loudly, he found no one to come to the door so he proceeded on around the house to the rear, following a faint trail.

He found everyone in the back yard enjoying the music, visiting, and eating; food—lots of it—sat on two long tables. As he entered the lighted area, someone shouted, "It's Mac!" and a little boy ran toward him, tackling his leg.

Grinning, McMurtry reached down and tousled the boy's hair. "How ya been, Elfigo?"

The little boy looked up at the Game Warden. "You wannna put me in the gazookus hold, Mac?" He referred to a wrestler's hold that McMurtry had placed many times on both boys while playing with them.

McMurtry laughed. "No, I reckon not right now, son.

I've got me a powerful hunger. How the vittles?"

Elfigo's brother appeared next to them. Jose's face was smiling. "Them veetles is good, Mac," he said, trying to emulate the Game Warden's speech.

"Wel-l-l now," McMurtry knelt in front of both boys, "I'm sure proud you boys are gettin' to see me tonight."

A voice behind him said, "Are you proud to see me, *Roberto?*"

He stood and turning saw Juanita. She was the prettiest woman he could ever recollect seeing in his entire life. Her dark hair hung to her shoulders. She wore a light beige jacket over a blue sweater and Levi jeans with comfortable black shoes. Her brown eyes were smiling.

It was his turn to smile. "You bet I am."

She took his arm, directing him toward the food and folks partying. An older Hispanic woman walked over to them as they headed for the food table. McMurtry could feel his stomach growl; he hadn't eaten since breakfast. With her gray hair pulled back into a tight roll at the nape of her neck, the woman wore wire-rimmed glasses, appeared tall and strong for a woman of her age. She wore black cotton slacks with a warm-looking white sweater. As they stood there the older Hispanic woman casually surveyed him from head to toe with piercing black eyes. She broke the silence, "So you're *Roberto*— ?"

"That's the rumor, ma'am." He smiled at her.

She did not return the smile, and finished the question, "—the *gringo* who has been seeing my niece?"

Juanita intervened, *"Sí, Tia. Este es Roberto* McMurtry, *mi novio."* She turned to McMurtry. "Thees ees *mi Tia Josie."*

McMurtry extended his hand. "Proud to make your acquaintance, ma'am."

The elderly woman did not shake his hand nor address

him. Instead, she turned to Juanita and said in rapid fire Spanish, "Why do you like these *gringos*? Do you not see that you should marry your own kind?"

Juanita's eyes blazed as she heatedly replied to the woman in Spanish then abruptly took McMurtry by the arm and steered him toward the food once more. He did not understand what had transpired in the conversation, but knew it had not been cordial. Watching as she literally threw food on his plate, he said softly, "Easy, Juanita. I got to eat that once you've throwed it all over my plate."

She stopped loading the plate, closed her eyes and exhaled slowly. "I'm so sorry, *Roberto*."

"No need to be." He placed his hands on her shoulders. "Not everybody's goin' to take a likin' to me." Shrugging, he said, "That's just the way it is in this ol' world. Come on, let's eat and enjoy the party."

Later, he met all the other family members who were very kind and respectful to him. McMurtry especially enjoyed visiting with Juanita's father, Pedro Flores. Flores had worked at the copper mine in Santa Rita for thirty-five years as an electrician. Señor Flores was not a tall man, but he did not appear short to the Game Warden either. Dark eyes and complexion with deep creases in his leathery face weathered by the outdoors and incessant sunshine, distinguished white hair, and a quiet easy way about him made Pedro Flores a favorite to McMurtry immediately.

Juanita's mother was shy, and although she did not converse at length with him, he felt comfortable and at home around her. The uncles were loud and boisterous, and of course full of *cerveza*. Tio Beto approached the Game Warden as he finished his second helping of tamales, rice, and re-fried beans with some *flan* for dessert.

Beto was the youngest brother of Pedro Flores, and unlike his older brother, *Beto* had never worked much at anything for very long during his life time. However, according to him, he was the expert on everything. Sporting a big belly that extended over his belt, he slapped McMurtry on the back and said, "*¿Qué pasa, guero?* What's happening, gringo?"

"Not much, *Beto*. Just fixin' to head back up to the Cliff Dwellings."

Beto laughed. "Haf a beer, man. Enjoy the party."

"No thanks on the beer. I got to drive the state truck."

"Suit yourself, man. I'm gonna haf another." *Beto* snorted and turned toward the ice chest.

McMurtry looked for Juanita as he tossed his paper plate in the trash and readied to leave. He thought he heard her voice inside the house so he moved in that direction. As he stepped inside from the back porch, he heard a man's voice. The man shouted loudly in Spanish then English. Stocky of build, he wore a cowboy straw hat, western shirt, Wrangler jeans and boots. A black pencil mustache made his head appear thinner than it actually was. His face was dark as was his close-cropped hair. McMurtry saw the man directed his comments to Juanita and her father.

Moving in closer to hear what was being said, McMurtry stopped just short of standing adjacent to Señor Flores.

Juanita's eyes were blazing as she stood toe to toe with the man and exchanged heated comments. The man switched to English. "I'll discipline my sons however I want, and neither you nor your two-bit father will tell me otherwise."

"Don' speek about *mi papa* that way."

The man sneered, "Shut up, you ... trashy—" and he shoved her back from him. A surprised McMurtry leapt forward and hit him hard below his left ear. Staggering backward, the man attempted to stand upright and as he turned, looking for his adversary, McMurtry swung his right with all his weight behind a punch that landed on the man's jaw. The man's head snapped back and he dropped to the floor.

Quiet blanketed the room full of stunned people who now peered down at the prostrate man lying still on the floor. Those same sets of eyes turned up toward the Game Warden. Total silence. Tio Beto burped and farted loudly.

McMurtry cleared his throat and asked as he addressed Juanita's father, "Say ... Pay-dro Floor-eez, just who in the hell is that feller yonder on the floor?"

"He ees my daughter Juanita's *ex-esposo, Roberto*," the elderly gentleman said softly with amusement in his dark eyes.

"Ez-pozo?" queried a cautious McMurtry as he leaned in close to the older man. "Jest exactly what is one o' them ez-posos anyways?"

Juanita answered, "He wass *mi* ... husband, *Roberto*. You know, before the divorce."

"Wel-l-l, I'll be dadjimmed." McMurty tucked his big, coarse hands inside the front of his coveralls. He winked at Juanita Flores, nodded politely to her father and headed for his truck.

CHAPTER FORTY

Wetzel sat on the porch of the rented apartment across from the Catholic Church. His new-found friend Robbie sat next to him in the quiet evening. Sunset arrived; the clouds in the west were accentuated by an orange glow of a tired sun about to call it a day. He pulled the collar up on his jacket as he felt the chill of the fall night creep slowly into his bones.

"Robbie, why don't you go inside where it's warm, uh?"

The little boy looked up at him, his big brown eyes smiling under long lashes. "Okay, Jack. Let's you and me play a game of checkers!"

Wetzel laughed as he stood. "You wanna get beaten *again*?"

Robbie's face took on a solemn look. "I'll get you this time. I know it."

Patting the boy's shoulders Wetzel opened the door to the apartment. "All right, but I've got to find your momma at the church first, okay?"

The little boy entered the apartment. "Okay, Jack."

"You close and lock the door, son." He motioned toward his border collie lying on a rug in the living room. "Stay with Montie. I'll be right back."

Only when he heard the door close and the dead bolt click did Wetzel step down off the porch and walk across the street toward the church.

***

The boy played with the dog for several minutes, throwing the stuffed toy across the room with Montie chasing to retrieve the toy and returning it to his friend. Robbie laughed hard at the dog running about, flipping the throw rug up and losing traction on the slick linoleum floor.

The dog stopped suddenly and ceased all activity. He cocked his head to one side, both ears perked at full attention. Then a slow, low growl began deep in his throat, he bared his fangs and barked loudly.

Robbie started for the door as he admonished the dog for being so loud, but the dog wouldn't let the boy past him. The boy tried again in vain as the growling dog kept him away from the door.

The little boy's brow furrowed as his lips pouted and he placed his hands on his hips. *"Montie, come here!"* he said with all the authority he could muster in his best command voice, but the dog remained in front of him always and wouldn't let him pass.

It was the boy's turn to cock his head sideways. Listening intently, he could not hear anything outside, but the longer he listened, he thought he heard someone try the door then soft footsteps outside the apartment. Images of the bad man dressed in black filled his head, the skin on his neck prickled and a severe shudder went through his little body followed by a fear greater than any he had ever known filled his whole being. He began to sob as he ran for the bedroom and hid under his bed. The growling dog followed, nestling against him.

CHAPTER FORTY-ONE

Maggie O'Brian-Garcia finished her prayers and lit a candle for her missing husband. As usual each evening, she had prayed not only for her Juan but also for her deceased father and now Doña Consuelo Vasquez. The church was very quiet and dark with only limited lighting to minimally illuminate the interior for those few, like herself, who visited at such a late hour. The church was never locked.

The large wooden door in the rear of the church creaked and she looked up to see her friend Wetzel appear, hat in hand. She smiled. He was the most polite man she had ever met. Walking quickly, she met him at the rear door.

His tanned face showed a worried expression as he said, "I didn't interrupt you, did I, Maggie?"

Pretty green eyes smiled at him. "No. Not at all, Jack. I was just leaving."

He followed her out of the church. The dusk had been swept away by the darkness of the night. Two cats screeched at each other as they fought down the street. They walked slowly down the steps in front of the church breathing in the clear, fresh air.

Wetzel spoke first. "Feels like snow."

"Maybeso. Thanksgiving's just around the bend."

"Do you mind sitting a spell on the steps?"

She looked quickly at him, unable to read his face in the dark of the evening. "Sure ... okay. How's right here?" she said, pointing at the bottom step near Market Street. He nodded and sat next to her. Reaching into his shirt pocket, he withdrew a Lucky Strike from the packet, stuck it into the corner of his mouth, and lit it with his silver lighter.

He smoked in silence for some time and she knew to say nothing. He would talk when it was time. They had come to know each other well lately. A bright red Dodge Charger cruised past, momentarily illuminating them in the headlights then disappeared down Yankee Street.

Wetzel tipped his Stetson back on his head with his thumb. He finished his cigarette and stubbed it out at the bottom of the step. Shifting uneasily on the concrete step, he said, "Maggie, what's to become of us, uh?"

She turned to face him, brows knitted, "What do you mean, Jack?"

"I mean *us*. You and me."

Hesitating before answering, she replied, "I'm sorry, did I do something to make you angry?"

"No, nothing like that ... I ...Maggie, I mean no disrespect for Juan, but I ... don't think he's coming back."

She gasped. "Oh—"

"It's been so long ... and ... God help me, I love you!"

Clasping her hands tightly in her lap, Maggie peered through the darkness of the evening at the young man sitting next to her. She saw he had dropped his hat, and distantly was reminded he had never done so in her presence prior to tonight. The evening breeze toyed at her red hair and chilled her as she sat on the cold concrete steps saying nothing.

He finally spoke. "I'm sorry, Maggie."

She reached out and gently touched his hands with hers. "Don't be, Jack. I'm ... I'm greatly honored you have an interest in me—that you love me is beyond my comprehension tonight."

Wetzel started to reply, but she placed her finger on his

lips. "I love you, too, my friend."

"But—?"

"I'm married."

A great sigh escaped his lips, and he took her in his arms and kissed her softly then hugged her tight to his breast. "Oh, Maggie, I know ... I know." He held her at arm's length and said softly to the heavens above, "Dear God, I mean no disrespect, only love for this woman, who I want to be my wife."

"Jack!" she cried out.

They sat awkwardly on the concrete steps, holding each other tightly not wanting to let go. A vehicle drove west on Market Street illuminating the couple as they sat in front of the church steps. The bright blue car passed them, moving very slowly, then stopped and backed up to where they sat. A young man leaned over into the passenger side of the 1962 Chevy Impala and said, "Hi there. I'm looking for a Maggie Garcia. Do you have any idea where she lives?"

Still holding each other, they said nothing. The young man gazed at one then the other, shrugged and started to drive away.

"I'm Maggie Garcia!" she shouted.

The brakes were applied firmly and the young man backed the car to his original location in front of the church. "Good," he replied with a smile, "You'll make my job easier tonight if you sign for this." He produced a brown envelope, holding it out to her from within the car.

"What is it?" she asked.

He paused then replied, "Oh, I'm sorry. I work for the Western Union." He pushed the envelope closer to her outstretched hand without getting out of the car. "It's a telegram from the U.S. Army, ma'am. And it's addressed to you."

CHAPTER FORTY-TWO

Police Chief Pete Thompson yawned loudly and stretched his arms above his head. He stood from his desk and looked at the clock on the wall. It was ten o'clock. He'd stayed later at work than he intended and it was definitely time to go home. His wife had called him twice, advising him that his supper was cold.

He'd done enough police work today for the citizens of Silver City. Yawning again he reached for his jacket hanging on the office wall peg. He put the jacket on, closed the open file on his desk and placed it in the metal file cabinet near the window. Taking a key from his heavy key chain on his duty belt, he securely locked it.

Walking down the small hallway, he opened the door to dispatch and stuck his head in. It was a weekday and only one dispatcher was working the night shift. The woman quickly placed a novel she had been reading down on the desk at her work station.

Thompson laughed to himself. *Hell, I don't give a damn if she reads her book when it's slow. Only that she answer the goddamned radio when officers call in.*

"How's it going tonight, Amanda?"

"Slow, sir. Very slow."

The old chief grinned as he chuckled. "That's the way I like it. Quiet and peaceful."

"Yes sir."

"You have a good evening. I'm going home." He closed the door and proceeded down the hallway to the back door.

Opening then closing the door, he stepped out in the clear, cold night. *Damn near forgot. Hell, it's Thanksgiving tomorrow. I can make up for all the suppers I've missed.* The stars literally danced in the sky overhead as a partial moon illuminated the parking lot behind the police station and showed him the way to his old truck he used to commute to work each day.

Yawning again, he fumbled with his keys, trying to find the one for his truck door and ignition. He sensed something first then he thought he heard a very subtle sound behind him close by. He shrugged it off to the wind that had begun to pick up. *I need to start wearing my heavier jacket. Damn, it's cold out here*.

He found the key and opened the door, the old metal door creaking in the quiet night. As he started to get into his truck, he heard the subtle noise again and turning nonchalantly toward the sound, he gasped. His officer awareness attempted to move from ground zero in the white zone all the way to red. It never made the transition.

"You!"

A soft popping sound, an impact then another just a second from the first. The first bullet tore through his chest, destroying his heart, and the second bullet entered his head between his eyes, blowing out the back part of his head. Chief Thompson dropped to the ground dead.

The assailant quickly picked up the shell casings, unscrewed the heavy silencer from the barrel of the semi-automatic pistol and slipped them into each jacket pocket. He turned and walked down Hudson Street for a block and disappeared into a side street. Standing there momentarily, he listened for any sound of alarm or pursuit. Hearing none, he smiled as he removed the black ski mask.

His right hand inadvertently moved in toward his torso, the thumb and forefinger touching as if cupping a cigarette in the hand with the little finger nervously flicking at the ashes on the end of a cigarette that did not exist.

***

It was Thanksgiving Day; the warm New Mexico sunshine on a clear, cloudless day felt reassuring to the old retired priest as he shuffled his tired feet up the steps and entered the mission church at San Lorenzo. The small village and church sat to the west and below the Black Range Mountains.

As dusk approached, the priest grunted as he genuflected in front of the altar in the little empty church. After making the sign of the cross, he began to pray, "*Padre nuestro, que estás en el cielo ...Our Father, who art in heaven ...*

He prayed tonight for resolution and an end to the Vietnam War, for peace in the world, for the poor parishioners who frequented the small church and struggled daily to make ends meet. And lastly, he prayed for the souls of those who had been slain in the Silver City area—a rancher, police officers, an old woman, and alas, the Police Chief. The old priest sighed; so much violence and death for such a small community. There was talk of drugs being the basis for the killings—drugs ... the devil's tools.

Outside, the shadow of the mountain slowly crept over the dwellings in the small village then the little church itself. Closing his eyes, he continued, "*...y líbranos del mal ... Amen. ...and deliver us from evil ... Amen.*

THE END

Other Books by John McLaughlin

Our Time in the Sun

This historically accurate account of an Old West group of lawmen, the Arizona Rangers, is an action-filled story complete with conflict, revenge, love, racism, and redemption in the Arizona Territory of 1903-04. Against the magnificent backdrop of the Southwest, the Rangers chase rustlers, help quell a major riot with miners in Morenci, and track the nefarious bandit, Indio Chacon, and his band of outlaws deep into the Sierra Madres in Mexico.

Elliott, a seasoned Ranger, struggles with his dark and violent past as he leads a contingent of Arizona Rangers stationed near the Mexican border. Along the way, Elliott finds time to mentor a young Ranger, Joaquin Campbell, who is short on law enforcement experience and life itself. Racism rears its ugly head as Campbell falls in love with a young Mexican woman.

This western adventure is the prequel to Red Sky at Morning.

"The man swallowed hard, placed his hands on his knees to catch a deep breath. He looked up at Elliott. 'I'm tellin' you to run, you damn fool! Bad men—kilt the bartender—stealin' money.' He licked his lips. 'I'm goin' ... to find ... ' Then he saw the silver stars on both men's shirts. 'Wait a minute—you are the law!'

Elliott dismissed the man, his eyes hard. 'Yessir ... thet's what we're here for.' He spoke to Joaquin without turning as he moved toward the door. 'When we go through the door—do it quick an' step to my left away from me.' With that he was gone, inside the saloon."

Red Sky at Morning

Young Joaquin Campbell has become an experienced Arizona Ranger and feels he's making a difference in establishing order in the territory; however, his wife doesn't share in those aspirations. Elliott, Joaquin's old friend and mentor, has married and resigned from the Arizona Rangers only to be called back repeatedly to assist the younger Rangers. His deadly skill as a gunman and his leadership experience is sorely needed.

Murderers have fled to Mexico; miners have revolted in Cananea, Mexico. American citizens have been murdered and families threatened. Ruthless, brutal smugglers are running guns across the border into Mexico to sell to the Yaqui Indians, and they will stop at nothing—

This action-packed story is set in the Arizona Territory of 1906-09, and it is the sequel to Our Time in the Sun. As such, it's a historically accurate account of an Old West group of lawmen, the Arizona Rangers.

"Elliott visualized the locations and fired at the first shooter, then snapped a quick shot at the second as he rolled on the floor to his right. Other guns boomed, bullets thudded into the wooden floor where he had been. They followed him as he rolled on the hard floor toward the back of the house. He winced as he felt a round hit him solidly in the back. It took the breath out of him. The firing continued. He lay on his back and fanned the hammer of his six-shooter as he aimed at the muzzle flashes from outside the windows. The resounding screams made his grim, tired face smile. 'Come and git it, boys! This ol' man ain't dead by a damn sight.'"

Purchase *Our Time in the Sun* and *Red Sky at Morning* on the web

www.johnmclaughlinbooks.com

Or visit with the author at

johnmclaughlinbooks@hotmail.com

CPSIA information can be obtained at www.ICGtesting.com
Printed in the USA
BVOW071157110512

289647BV00002B/2/P

9 780615 545189